The Lost Horse

The Lost Horse

Elaine Heney

The Connemara Adventure Series

The Forgotten Horse

The Show Horse

The Mayfield Horse

The Stolen Horse

The Adventure Horse

The Lost Horse

The Coral Cove Series

The Riding School Connemara Pony

The Storm and the Connemara Pony

The Surprise Puppy and the Connemara Pony

The Castle Charity Ride and the Connemara Pony

Horse Books for Kids

P is for Pony – ABC Alphabet Book for Kids 2+

Listenology for Kids age 7-14

Horse Care, Riding and Training for kids 6-11

Horse Puzzles, Games & Brain Teasers for kids 7-14

Horse Books for Adults

Equine Listenology Guide

Dressage Training for Beginners

The Listenology Guide to Bitless Bridles

Ozzie, the Story of a Young Horse

Conversations with the Horse

Horse Anatomy Coloring Book

"Listening to the horse is the most important thing we can do"

Elaine Heney

First Edition August 2022 | Published by Grey Pony Films

www.greyponyfilms.com

Table of contents

About Elaine Heney

Elaine Heney is an Irish horsewoman, film producer at Grey Pony Films, #1 best-selling author, and director of the award-winning 'Listening to the Horse™' documentary. She has helped over 120,000+ horse owners in 113 countries to create great relationships with their horses. Elaine's mission is to make the world a better place for the horse. She lives in Ireland with her horses Ozzie & Matilda. Find all Elaine's books at **www.writtenbyelaine.com**

Online horse training courses

Discover our series of world-renowned online groundwork, riding, training programs and apps. Visit Grey Pony Films & learn more: **www.greyponyfilms.com**

Chapter 1

Clodagh giggled as Rachel took the flashlight and held it under her chin, pulling a face as she prepared to tell the ending of yet another spooky story. They had made a sort of tent in Clodagh's bedroom, pulling a few sheets over her chair, desk and bed, filling it with an assortment of cushions and bedding so they could chat and sleep in it too. Ma had even let them have a few snacks; on the understanding they were not to be eaten at midnight because they all needed to be asleep by then.

"And all they found in the morning," Rachel said. "Was a single boot!"

Beth laughed as she stuffed a crisp in her mouth, while Clodagh remained quiet. While she loved spooky, creepy tails, she often found that her imagination ran wild after hearing them, and even far-fetched stories like the one Rachel had just told, made her shiver.

"That has to be the worst story, I mean come on, the janitor was a werewolf, he couldn't get a better job?" Beth giggled.

Rachel smiled and shook her head. "I swear, it's true, I heard it at my old school!"

"Right, after twilight and all that stuff, a werewolf becomes a janitor. He'd be like some movie star or something," Beth went on.

"Ohh that reminds me," Rachel smiled. She looked over at Clodagh. "Have you heard from Ash? I bet he has a few good ghost stories from all the places he's visited?"

Clodagh nodded as she crunched another salty crisp. "He's really excited about the Halloween party and all the things Mrs. Fitz and Dad have come up with. He wanted to be here all week to help, but I think he said at best it would be Thursday when he gets here. He doesn't really have school holidays like us, so it's just when whatever he's filming ends."

"It's a shame there isn't anyone for him to ride," Beth said. "It would be nice to all hack out together, go for a canter up in the forty-acre like when he was here filming. Maybe we could ask Sandra if he could lend a horse for an hour from the riding school?"

"That's an idea." Clodagh smiled, imagining herself on Ozzie cantering next to her friends all together. "It would be nice."

"I could ask," Rachel said suddenly looking much less cheerful. "I have to go over tomorrow on the way home anyway."

"How come?" Beth asked, sneaking another crisp.

Rachel looked almost uncomfortable. Clodagh frowned. "Rach, what is it?"

Rachel took a deep breath. "Grandad's retiring."

"Retiring, what does that mean? Is he giving up the farm?" Beth asked, her face suddenly serious. Clodagh felt her heart sink. Rachel kept Dancer, her little black pony, at her Grandad's farm. If he sold up it would mean she would have to keep her somewhere else.

Rachel shook her head. "Mum doesn't want it, but," Rachel bit her lip. "I heard them talking and I told him I did, that I'd run it, if he could keep going until I finish school. Mum said I was being silly and I got pretty mad." Clodagh glanced at Beth, but neither said anything, waiting patiently for Rachel to go on. "I, I mean, she brought us here, to the farm, right? She said it was the best place for us and then she was saying she didn't want it and that I would be silly to take it over and when I told her it wasn't silly, she said I needed to go to university like she did and make something of myself. I pointed out that she works at the local library. I don't think she was pleased, but Grandad started to laugh. That didn't help Mum's mood at all."

"What did Mel say?" Clodagh asked.

"Mum stormed off and Grandad asked me if I really meant it? If I wanted to be a farmer? I told him not really, at least, not like he is. I think the farm could be much more than what it is."

"What do you mean?" Beth asked.

They instinctively huddled closer together. Surrounded by the darkness of the night, illuminated only by the little torch, it felt like they were some secret society swapping clandestine tales. It seemed fitting and exciting.

"Well, I'd like to do more like what farmer Bob does. Have a farm shop, but get lots more local people's crafts and produce in it, not just from our farm, but from others too. Maybe do some pick your own and perhaps a petting place, you know, for kids."

"That sounds amazing!" Clodagh said.

"Yeah," Rachel beamed. "There's nothing like that around here, but Dad took me to one once. It had tractor rides and a café. There was this really cool playpark too, like all wooden with slides. I think it would be great, local families could go, but now the manor is here too and doing holidays, it could get tourists."

"It's the sort of thing Ma advertises in the hallway," Clodagh mused, thinking about the little plastic rack Ma had at the entrance to the

B&B filled with local leaflets for day trips and places of interest. Rachel nodded as she grabbed a crisp.

"Does your Mum know that?" Beth asked her. "Your plan I mean."

Rachel shook her head. "She wouldn't even listen, but Grandad did. He loves the idea, but he said he can't keep going as much as he'd like too. I think it was him hurting his ankle that did it, Gran says he isn't getting any younger and he needs to start slowing down."

"The words Mel and slowing down don't fit very well together," Clodagh mused.

"That's what he said," Rachel agreed.

Clodagh glanced up sadly at Rachel, it seemed like too good an idea just to be squashed like an over-ripe pumpkin. "Isn't there any way to keep the farm?"

"Oh, Grandad isn't selling," Rachel said, surprising them. "After he heard my idea, he rang around a bit and decided to rent his fields to some of the other local farms. He's keeping the house and renting everything else. He talked to Mum and told her straight that if I wanted it when I'm old enough he'll help me take over and if I decide I don't then he'll sell it on. He even made an appointment with his solicitor to make it legal."

"Wow," Clodagh said. Rachel smiled.

"Wait, did you say he's renting everything?" Beth asked.

Rachel's face fell again and she nodded. "I need to find another place to keep Dancer, at least for now. Grandad said I can have as long as we need, but eventually..." she trailed off.

"That's why you want to talk to Sandra," Beth stated.

Rachel nodded. "At least there I can ride with Clodagh most days." She smiled and Clodagh did too. "Besides, it's not as bad there now. Sandra and Charlotte are much nicer since we saved Gracie."

"Ugh, this is too depressing," Beth said flopping back on an oversized cushion and tipping a few crumbs from the can of crisps they had been eating into her mouth. "It's the autumn holidays, Halloween is coming, we should be talking about candy, pumpkins, costumes and spooky ghosts."

"Speaking of," Rachel said. "Did you ask her? Mrs. Fitz, did you ask her about the ghost?"

Clodagh smiled. Back in the summer she had discovered that the old manor, in whose gatehouse she lived, had its very own ghost story. It had never occurred to her that the manor could be haunted and yet, somehow it seemed fitting that it should be. The large old grey manor had always had a strange, almost magical air to it. Clodagh had felt like she had glimpsed hints of it growing up, but it hadn't been until Ozzie had arrived that she had really felt something mystical about the place. Horses made the manor somehow come to life, as if they magically connected with it, drawing out the past. So, how fitting it had been to discover that the ghost story connected with the manor was also connected to a horse.

"Well?" Beth asked, sitting up.

"I asked her," Clodagh smiled. "Do you want to hear it?"

"Yes!" Rachel and Beth said together and then giggled.

Clodagh smiled and grabbed the torch. "It all happened in the 1700's." Clodagh began, remembering back to when Mrs. Fitz had almost gleefully told her the tale as they sat in the manor library drinking tea and watching rain pelt against the huge windows. "Long before the manor as we know was built. Back then there was an older house standing where the manor is now. You can even see parts of it in the basement. Mrs. Fitz promised to show me it sometime."

"Wow, I didn't even know there was a basement," Rachel sighed.

Clodagh nodded. "I didn't either, Mrs. Fitz said it was used as a wine cellar and pantry. Anyway, the manor was owned by a really wealthy family. The lord was a supporter of the Queen, but his daughter, Lilly, fell in love with a young Catholic man who refused to go to protestant church and who was branded a recusant."

"What's that?" Rachel asked.

"Mrs. Fitz said it was a bit complicated, but basically under Queen Elizabeth everyone had to go to Anglican services. Some people still were Catholic and pretty much it was ok, so long as they went to the Anglican church publicly. Some people though refused, and they were punished. They were known as recusants. Anyway, Lilly planned to escape and leave with her true love and to go to Spain where they'd get married. Mrs. Fitz said that in some of the legends the young man had family there who were wealthy and would help them. Lilly had everything planned, right down to how to get her favourite horse, Veillantif, to Spain, because she wouldn't leave without him. On a dark, foggy night in October, she slipped out of the manor and rode Veillantif to meet her true love."

"So romantic," Rachel sighed.

"But her father had uncovered the plot and sent men to arrest the young man. He didn't want his daughter married to someone like that. As Lilly arrived, she watched in horror as he was arrested and dragged away to who knows what fate. Her father appeared and told her she would be going home and would marry someone he chose."

"Glad he's not my Dad," Beth huffed.

"It gets worse," Clodagh went on. "As he came closer, he said he'd sell Veillantif too. It was all too much for Lilly and she spun around on Veillantif, riding heedlessly into the foggy night. No one ever saw her again. Some of the legends say she was so grief stricken she rode Veillantif off the sheer drop behind the manor."

"Would a horse do that?" Rachel asked.

"I doubt Mav would," Beth said.

"The tales say he was so loyal the thought of being taken from Lilly was too much for the horse to bear and so he willingly died with her." Clodagh said.

"OH," Rachel put her hand over her heart. "That's so sad."

"Sometimes in the story though, they get lost in the fog and just ride off by accident," Clodagh added.

"That'd be Dancer," Rachel said. "She'd do something like that, oh, whoops, sorry Rachel didn't see that cliff there."

They all laughed. "Mrs. Fitz's favourite version has the nicest ending though. It's pretty odd though."

"What?" Beth asked, her eyes dancing.

"Well, a couple of the stories say that the fairy folk were out riding that night and saw Lilly. The king of the fairies, Oberon, saw how distressed she was and revealed himself to her. He asked the girl what was wrong and she told him. He offered her and Veillantif sanctuary in his court and she agreed on the condition that should her true love be spared, she would be allowed to return to him. Oberon agreed to allow her to come to the land of man every night for one week a year to seek her true love and if she found him, she could stay, if not, she would return to the kingdom of the fairy."

"And?" Beth asked leaning further forward.

"Well, every now and then, around this time of year, people say they see a lady dressed in a flowing dress, her hair long and loose, riding heedlessly around the manor on a white horse. She seems to look for something, calling out her true love's name, hoping that this year she will find him and join him, free to be together forever."

Rachel shuddered a little. "Ok, that's better than the werewolf janitor."

"I'll say," Beth giggled.

"It's not so creepy really," Clodagh said, "I mean, I don't think I'd feel too worried meeting Lilly. She sounds nice, her story's sad though."

"I wonder if there's any truth to it," Beth said.

"Oh, for sure," Rachel smiled. "I mean, we see the fairy's tramping through the woods on every ride," she smiled.

Beth rolled her eyes. "Ha, ha. I mean I wonder if Lilly was a real person, maybe her story is made up, but she could be based on a real historical figure. Like Robin Hood or Merlin."

"Merlin?" Rachel smiled.

"There's some historical figures that probably formed the basis of his character," Beth said. "Sarah is doing English Literature at uni, she told me, they did a whole paper on it."

"It would be interesting to find out," Clodagh mused. "But I doubt we could ever find any records from that far back."

"I wonder what happened after Lilly disappeared?" Beth mused. "It feels so friendly and warm, I can't imagine a man like Lilly's dad being in it."

"Mrs. Fitz said something similar. She said there were a few old tales that said he went mad and that after that the manor was sold on. The farm was built and then the old manor was eventually burnt down and left to rot for a while before being replaced with the manor we have now. You know what's weird though?"

"What?" Rachel asked.

"According to Mrs. Fitz, our manor was built by one of her ancestors called John Fitzgerald. His wife was a keen horse rider and you'll never guess what she was called."

"Lilly!" They said at once. Clodagh nodded.

"Girls, lights out now." Ma's voice drifted into the room. They sighed.

"I'll close the curtains, you guy's sort out the cushions," Clodagh said, wiggling out of their den.

She padded across her room towards the window. The night was a dark midnight blue studded with diamond stars, a full bright moon hung in it, illuminating the paddock down below her room, across the drive.

Clodagh looked out at the shadowed shape of the manor, sat in the silver moonlight. It certainly looked magical and haunted all at the same time on nights like this. She was just closing the curtains and taking a final look at Ozzie, still grazing in the dew-covered paddock, when something caught her eye. Had she seen a white horse by the paddock fence?

She looked up sharply and shook her head when she saw nothing but the dark woods, their thinning branches gently waving in a slight breeze. She finished closing the curtains and hurried back to the den, glad she wasn't sleeping alone that night. Listening to those spooky stories had gotten to her.

Clodagh snuggled into her space in the den and Rachel frowned at her. "You, ok?"

"Yeah, I think the spooky stories are getting to me."

"Me too," Rachel said. "I'm never sleeping again."

They glanced over at Beth who was already asleep and giggled a little as they both settled down.

Chapter 2

Clodagh balanced carefully on the step ladder. Holding onto the top of it she reached up to hang the end of the garland she had in her hand onto the curtain pole in the manor library. The garland was made up of big black and orange-shaped pumpkins and bats. On the other side of the room, Beth hung up a matching one above the windows there, carefully hooking the end of the string over the finial.

"It's not very creepy, is it?" she said as she looped up the string.

Clodagh smiled. She knew Mrs. Fitz's big Halloween plan involved much more than the library, but she hadn't told them that just yet, it was all a big surprise. The original plan had been to hold a small party for guests in the library, but that had changed after Mrs. Fitz had discovered the parish hall had cancelled their kid's party. She had come to Dad with a plan Clodagh thought was brilliant. She couldn't wait to see everything all done and finished, it was going to be amazing. It had been hard not to tell them all what was going on, but Mrs. Fitz had made her promise to say nothing until she was absolutely sure they could do it and she had confirmed that morning everything was perfect.

Clodagh wondered if she should tell them now. She glanced over at the older lady, who was arranging a pumpkin on one of the bookshelves. Mrs. Fitz gave her a knowing look and winked. Rachel dropped a roll of fake police tape with the word CAUTION printed on it in a funny gloopy-looking font.

"Sorry," she said, rushing to pick it up.

"Are you ok?" Clodagh asked.

Rachel sighed and sat down on one of the chairs, fiddling with one the end of a paper chain they had made earlier that morning. It was very clear she wasn't alright.

"I don't know, I guess I'm worried about going down to Briary later," she said.

"Maybe you should pop down now, we'll be ok here," Beth said. "You might feel better once you've been."

"Are you going for a lesson?" Mrs. Fitz asked. Rachel shook her head sadly.

"Mel's retiring and renting out the farm, Rachel's going to ask about livery," Clodagh said.

Mrs. Fitz glanced over at Clodagh and frowned. "I'm fairly sure Sandra's full. She was asking around about extra grazing last week."

Rachel's face fell even further. "What am I going to do? I don't want to have to take her miles away. Mum's so busy, she'll never have time to take me to see her every day." Her voice cracked a little and she swallowed hard. Clodagh started to climb down the ladder, feeling the need to be close to her friend.

"I don't see why you just don't bring her over here, keep Ozzie company," Mrs. Fitz said, turning the pumpkin a little bit. She tilted her head, frowned, and then turned it back again until it was perfect.

Rachel's head shot up and she stared at Mrs. Fitz for a second, her eyes dancing. "Really? Here?" she asked, then she faltered, she bit her lip. "How much would I need to pay?"

"Oh, I don't know," Mrs. Fitz said, pausing. "How does £80 a month sound?"

"A lot cheaper than Briary," Rachel beamed.

"You'll need to get your own hay and bedding though if you use one of the boxes when the weather's really bad."

"Of course!" Rachel said, still in shock.

"Well, that's settled then. Now, do hurry along stringing up those chains, we still have downstairs to sort out." Mrs. Fitz said.

"Downstairs?" Beth asked, frowning as she looked around herself. "Aren't we there already?"

Mrs. Fitz laughed a little. "There's still a little bit more down to explore and it's going to take some work to sort out," she said as she headed towards the door. "I'm going to gather a few more pumpkins. Once you girls have finished the library, we'll go take a look."

"I can't believe it," Rachel said as soon as she was gone. She jumped up with a squeal, spilling the paper chains into a heap as she did. Clodagh smiled broadly. It would be great for Ozzie to have some real company and Dancer! They could ride with Rachel any time they liked. "I need to ring Grandad."

"Here," Beth handed her phone to Rachel.

"Thanks," she said rushing into the hallway to call Mel.

"What did Mrs. Fitz mean by downstairs?" Beth asked, squinting at Clodagh.

Clodagh smiled as she scooped up the paper chains and started to hang them on the bookshelves with her. Rachel came back in still smiling and handed Beth back her phone.

"What did he say?" Clodagh asked.

"He asked how soon could he load her up and bring her here?" she laughed. "Apparently she's been chasing the sheep around and round the paddock today, just for fun."

They all giggled at the thought of Dancer trying to play tag with the poor sheep and Mel shouting irately from the window for her to stop, while simultaneously trying not to laugh.

"Clodagh, downstairs?" Beth asked again, snapping her fingers in front of Clodagh's face to bring her back to reality. Clodagh smiled and pushed Beth's hand away gently.

Clodagh sighed. "Oh, alright. Mrs. Fitz had the idea to sort of hold two parties at the manor. Anyone who is really young will come in here." She looked around the library with a smile. All of the decorations were cute, Halloween-themed ones. Smiling pumpkins, paper chains in orange, black and purple, an inflatable ghost suspended from the ceiling, and a string of pumpkin lights hung around the fireplace. "We're going to move the big table out and take up the rug, there'll be party games and some cheesy Halloween music. Nothing really scary. Ma's doing a few snacks too, but they'll be next door in the dining room. She suggested we make some creepy Halloween lemonade, adding green food colouring too."

"That sounds nice," Rachel said.

Clodagh nodded. "There was going to be a kid's party in the Parish Hall doing that sort of thing, but they had a burst pipe, the halls a mess, so she offered to move it here. They're bringing over some more things later in the week as well as supervising the kids. I think Mrs. Fitz said it's going to be fancy dress; it should be great."

"It's nice of Mrs. Fitz to step in like that," Beth said.

"The manor is doing so much better financially now; I think she wants to share the joy. Besides, I think she really likes to see the manor busy, like it's meant to be I suppose," Clodagh said. It was certainly true. Since they had converted some of the manor and the adjoining old farm into holiday lets, the whole place seemed more, well, alive.

"So, where's the second party?" Rachel asked.

Clodagh smiled. "Remember the ghost story?"

"Yeah?" Beth said confused.

"This manor was built on the foundations of the old one. The original basement is underneath. It hasn't been used for ages, it's full of junk. Mrs. Fitz wants to clean it out and decorate it for a grown-up party, with cool spooky decorations and everything. She had someone come out and make sure it was safe. They must have said yes." Clodagh smiled. She was really excited to see another part of the manor she hadn't even known existed and the fact it was linked to the ghost story made it even more exciting.

"That is so awesome!" Rachel said bouncing on the balls of her feet.

"Let's hurry and finish up so we can go take a look," Beth said grabbing another paper chain.

"Wait," Rachel said. "Are the parties going to be at exactly the same time? I wouldn't mind popping in here to check it out," she smiled.

Clodagh smiled too. "Not exactly. The kid's party is going to be on straight after the pumpkin trail ride, we're setting up, so it'll start about 5 and finish at about 7, which is when the grown-up party will start. I thought we could come and volunteer to help out here for an hour after the ride and then go get changed for the party in the cellar."

"Sounds good to me," Beth said. "So long as we can get changed at yours."

"Sure," Clodagh smiled.

Clodagh went to help her but stopped as she saw Ozzie through the library window. He was trotting across to the woods that bordered his paddock. Clodagh frowned and wandered over peering out to see what he was looking at, but try as she might there was nothing.

"What is it?" Rachel asked.

"Ozzie, he went trotting over to the woods," Clodagh replied, still staring to see something.

"It's probably Sam walking Basil," Beth said, hanging up the chain. Clodagh smiled a little relieved, of course, Ozzie loved to trot along the fence next to Basil when he went for a walk. That was bound to be it, Dad would be busy today getting the manor ready for the party too. Ma was sorting new guests for the B&B, so obviously Sam would offer to walk Basil. She was spooking herself again, with a smile she glanced once more at Ozzie and then grabbed the end of the chain, looping it onto the bookcase.

"Let's go check the basement," she said.

*

Mrs. Fitz pulled open an old door opposite the main stairs. Clodagh had seen it before and always assumed it was a coat room, but no, it was the entrance to the old basement. Mrs. Fitz looked over her shoulder at them and smiled. She flicked a switch on the wall and a bare lightbulb fizzed into life revealing a narrow, yellow sandstone passage, stone steps leading down into the original manor.

"Shall I go first?" she asked. They nodded to her, none of them able to say anything. Mrs. Fitz chuckled to herself as she took hold of a thick rope anchored to the wall by black iron rings and began to descend the stairs.

Clodagh followed Mrs. Fitz, trailing her hand along the coarse rope, her fingers grazing the stone sometimes. It grew colder the further down they went and Clodagh wondered if it may be a bit cold for her witch costume. Come to think of it, she'd need to try it on and make sure it still fitted. She made a mental note to dig it out when she got home and check.

The stairs ended and Mrs. Fitz stopped, her hand poised over an old-fashioned peg-shaped switch that somehow managed to look modern against the stonework.

"Ready?" she asked.

"Yes," Clodagh answered for them all excitedly.

Mrs. Fitz snapped down the switch and light flooded the old cellars. Clodagh gasped. In front of her was a wide corridor off which were four large arches.

"Originally," Mrs. Fitz explained as she walked forwards. "These arches were the entrances to four separate rooms, two wine cellars, and two pantries." They followed her forwards until they were in the middle of the corridor. Clodagh could see where the old walls had probably once divided the place, but now it was just one large room on each side of the corridor. "My father took the walls out during the war. Turned the cellars into a bomb shelter." She patted the walls. "Always said it was the safest place to be during a raid," she sighed. "Afterwards the rooms were used to store old wood and paint. Your father cleared it all out," she said to Clodagh. "And I had it checked for damp, vermin, and so on. I think it will do rather nicely for a Halloween party, don't you?"

"Oh yes," Clodagh said, turning around herself.

"So, are we doing spooky decorations here?" Beth asked looking a little unsure.

"I thought we might, but I'm sensing you have an idea," Mrs. Fitz said.

Beth walked around the room, dipping through the arches and checking out the space, muttering as she did. She spun on her heel and looked at them. "It's just, well, I'm not sure skeletons in the corner and creep pictures staring at you would work. It looks too nice, too classy for plastic stuff."

"She might have a point," Rachel said, nodding. "I mean it would be cool and creepy, but it somehow seems wrong to stick fake gory stuff here."

Clodagh smiled. "What if we did something a little different? We could recreate the old ghost story of Lilly. Get fake cobwebs and put them on decent candle sticks, make it look like we just uncovered the basement and it had been left this way since Lilly became a ghost!"

"OHH, we could even add some fairy touches, like as if she were having a party for the hunt she met!" Rachel added.

"Yes, yes, that sounds lovely," Mrs. Fitz said. "We could add some fairy lights to make it dimmer, and put some fake candles in the sconces."

Clodagh looked and realised there were metal brackets on the wall waiting to hold candles as they once had.

"I wonder if we could hide the trestle table with a cloth so it looks like a medieval one?" Clodagh mused.

"I should think your Ma could do that easily," Mrs. Fitz said. "And I think there are some old chairs we might dot about in the garage."

"It's a shame we can't get someone to pretend to be Lilly, her true love and Oberon," Beth said.

"Wouldn't that be fun?" Rachel said. "We could ask Ash?"

Clodagh laughed. "I'm not sure even Ash is a good enough actor to play Lilly."

"Funny," Rachel wrinkled her nose.

"You and Sam could," Clodagh suggested looking at Beth.

"I'm struggling to get Sam not to come dressed as something from the world of warcraft. I have no chance," Beth sighed.

"It's a lovely idea, but first we need this space sorted out," Mrs. Fitz said. "We'll need to get rid of any real cobwebs, give everything a clean and find some decorations, furniture and so on. I suggest we go on a bit of a scavenger hunt for things that might be useful." She handed Clodagh a notebook and pencil. "You girls start downstairs, most of the things on display there aren't too valuable or of sentimental value. Whatever might be useful make a note of. You should check the garages too. Then we'll regroup and do the attic together. Once we have what we need we can start cleaning it up. Alright."

"Alright!" They smiled and raced off to explore the manor and find the perfect things to make the perfect manor Halloween. As they jogged up the stairs, Clodagh paused and looked back at the basement that had once belonged to Lilly. She had wondered if Lilly had ever been a real person or if the ghost story was just a made-up tale, but looking at that space, she was more certain than ever that at least part of the manor ghost story was true. She smiled as Mrs. Fitz flicked off the light and began to follow her up the stairs.

Chapter 3

Ash waved at Clodagh through the video link, his hand freezing a little as the signal tried to catch up. Clodagh smiled and waved back. Clearly, he was sitting on a beach somewhere much warmer and sunnier than she was. Outside the grey sky had been threatening to rain for a few hours now and while Ash was sitting in a t-shirt, she was wearing a thick baggy, grey sweater.

"Is it cold there?" Ash laughed.

"Yes," she replied with a giggle. "I'm guessing it's not where you are."

"Not bad huh?" he said, angling his phone so she could see the whole beach, the cool blue/green waves lapping on the golden sands. "I'd still rather be where you are though, how's the decorating going?"

"It's really cool," Clodagh said thinking about how things were going. With the help of Rachel and Beth, she had found tons of stuff to decorate the basement. They had cleaned and swept out the whole place with Mrs. Fitz and Ma, while Dad and Sam had started bringing in furniture and decorations. Beth had discovered a little alcove at the back of one of the rooms, and by hanging up some fabric they had managed to hide a little sound system so they could play music and creepy noises. Alongside some fake cobwebs, Dad had found a projector online, so they could have spooky images shown on the walls. Rachel had set up all the sconces with fake candles that flickered. Sam had the great idea of decorating the hallway around the basement entrance with skeletons, crows, and pumpkins, so people were a little creeped out before they went downstairs. Everything was coming together brilliantly, she only wished she could show Ash what they had done. "I wanted to show you, but Sam says there's no way I'd get a signal."

Ash frowned. "From the manor? The production crew had a signal before."

Clodagh smiled. "Not from the basement."

"Basement?" Ash asked.

Clodagh nodded. She explained all about the kid's party and how they had decided to hold the grown-up party in the basement instead, using the old ghost story as inspiration.

"That sounds so cool, but I'm kind of bummed I'll miss the apple bobbing," he smiled.

"Oh, no way, we're not missing apple bobbing. We can go to both parties. The kid's party is going to be right after our trail ride and finish as the grown up one starts; we're volunteering to help out with the kids party for an hour. I think the kids would get a huge kick out of having movie actor Ash Hutchins appear at their party," Clodagh smiled.

"About that," a smirk crossed Ash's face. "You think you could host one more guest?"

"Who?" Clodagh asked.

"Me!" Melissa's face popped up on the screen next to her brothers. "I had the production crew move my schedule around a bit so I can come!"

"That's amazing!" Clodagh smiled. "Sure, you can come, if there are no rooms at the B&B you can bunk in with me and the girls!"

Melissa smiled and looked around conspiratorially. "Actually, I think I'd prefer that. Ash said you were having a trail ride too. Any chance we could tag along?"

Clodagh smiled; she'd been hoping that Ash would ask that. She'd been down to Briary earlier to talk the whole thing over with Sandra and they had come up with a great plan.

"I think we can do that. Sandra is going to take part in the whole celebrations and let some of her horses be used on the ride. Lots of her students want to do it, but they have to be over ten and good riders since it's going to be in the dark. I already asked if Ash could use a horse, I'll call her and see if she has someone you could ride."

"Fantastic, I guess it's a paid ride, let us know what we'll owe Sandra," Melissa said.

"I will," Clodagh smiled.

"I heard you telling Ash about the basement. That sounds so awesome," Melissa said.

"It really is, I tried to persuade Sam and Beth to turn up as Lilly and her true love and get Dad to dress as Oberon, but Sam wouldn't do it and Dad says he's too busy sorting out the kid's games." A sudden thought crossed her mind and she smiled at Ash and Melissa. "You guys want to do it?"

"Be Ash's true love?" Melissa stuck her tongue out. "Barf, no thank you" Ash elbowed her but the pair giggled.

"Like you're a catch," Ash giggled.

Clodagh laughed. "Well, just some costumes then."

"Oh, I am raiding the wardrobe this afternoon," Melissa giggled. "Do you have yours?"

Clodagh glanced down a little and shook her head a little sadly. "No. I was going to wear my witch costume, but I kind of outgrew it. I'll sort something out though. Beth and Rachel said they'd help. I just have to finish organising some things first. I was sort of hoping to see if Angela, that bought Troy from the film, might come and bring the trail riders to the manor in the old carriage, but I couldn't get through to her on the phone before. Mrs. Fitz says she'll try later."

"This is going to be the best Halloween," Melissa squeaked.

"It really is, but we need to go if we want to finish up here and make our flight. We'll see you Thursday," Ash said with another wave.

Clodagh smiled. "See you then."

The screen flashed off and Clodagh closed the laptop lid with a sigh. She glanced at the wood burner wondering if Dad was going to light it for the first time that autumn tonight. It had looked so lovely on the beach that Ash and Melissa were on, but she could understand what Ash had meant when he said he'd prefer to be at the manor. Sunshine, beach, and sea just didn't seem, well, Halloween-ey. The manor, the grey sky, and the almost bare trees fit the season much better. Instinctively she glanced out of the window at the dark grey clouds. She'd hoped to hack out with Ozzie, but looking at the sky she knew they'd be getting very wet if they went too far. Maybe they should do a bareback tour of the paddock. Smiling at the thought, she put the laptop onto the coffee table and headed off to gather her coat, boots, grooming kit, bridle, and hat.

*

When Clodagh stepped outside, she discovered it wasn't quite as chilly as it had been earlier. The grey clouds were still blocking the sun, but the breeze had died down, so it didn't feel as cool. She jogged down the drive of the B&B, her boots crunching on the yellow stone chippings as she went. Surprisingly Ozzie wasn't at the gate and she frowned as she crossed the tarmac and wove through the trees wondering what he was up to.

During the summer, when the grass had been rich, she had only let him graze the lower half of the paddock, but as it had grown colder, she'd opened the gate in the middle of the field so he had the whole thing to wander through. She had expected him to be huddled up in the top corner by the manor. He'd taken a liking to the spot since they'd been setting up for Halloween. He could stare through the library window at them and had the shelter of both the trees from the woods and the big rhododendron bushes of the manor garden too. Clodagh secretly suspected Mrs. Fitz snuck him a carrot every evening too, late on when she locked up. A few times she'd found crumbs around the little iron gate opposite the big barn doors.

When she reached the gate though she saw he was halfway up the field looking into the woods again as if he was looking for something. Clodagh shivered. The story of Lilly and Veillantif flashed into her head and she swallowed hard.

"Ozzie!" she called. It came out quieter than usual as if she were slightly afraid her shout would call the attention of someone, or something, else as well as the little grey pony. Ozzie looked over his shoulder at her, glanced back at the woods, and then began to amble over towards her. Clodagh scolded herself mentally, she was being silly, letting the old ghost story get to her. She wasn't sure what she was scared of anyway. Whatever Ozzie was looking at, it didn't seem to frighten him.

Ozzie reached the gate and she scratched his neck, rubbing her cold fingers through his soft, thick, warm coat. She glanced at the sky overhead and sighed.

"How about a nice little bareback ride around the paddock for tonight huh?" Ozzie snorted and tossed his head in agreement.

Clodagh climbed over the gate and fished a brush out of her bag, hanging it on the gate as she went. She quickly groomed him, brushing any dirt from his coat, mane, and tail.

"There, that's better," she smiled. Just being with Ozzie like this was chasing the spooky feelings away. "You know I'm creeping myself out right?" He glanced at her and she was sure he did a horse-y eye roll, it made her smile. "I know, I'm being silly." She began to slip Ozzie's bridle on. "I mean, even if Lilly is a ghost and she's really riding around here, we shouldn't be scared of her, right?"

Ozzie seemed to contemplate what she was saying as she climbed onto the fence and slipped onto his back. He stood still as Clodagh settled herself onboard. She never really had to use her reins, or even her legs when they rode bareback. It was enough just to think about moving and turning which way she wanted. They set off around the paddock, Ozzie ambling as usual.

"Lilly and Veillantif are like us really. So, if she was real, she'd see that and be nice to us," Clodagh justified to herself. She shuddered though, a ghost, while she may be a nice one, would still be a ghost. "I think I'll feel better when Dancer and Rachel are here."

It was true. Clodagh never felt safer than with Ozzie; she was certain he'd keep her safe. But if Rachel were here, she'd tell Clodagh to stop worrying and thinking about ghosts and spooky tales. Dancer would also be there in the paddock with Ozzie, keeping him company at night when Clodagh was tucked up in bed.

They had ridden around the bottom part of the paddock a couple of times, but now they headed up the field, following the woods that inclined towards the manor. Clodagh looked at it, a dark grey stone shape against the lighter grey sky. The manor had always looked gloomy and unkept before Ozie had arrived. Now it had a strange quality to it as if somehow it seemed proud of itself once more.

She was just about to tell Ozzie about how the decoration was going when the sound of a horse whinny made her freeze. Evidently, Ozzie had heard the shout too. He stopped in his tracks, his head going up, little grey ears twisting around like radars. Clodagh swallowed and rubbed his neck a little.

"Probably one of Briary's ponies," she tried to laugh, but it sounded hollow. The sound hadn't sounded like it had come from the direction of the riding school at all. Then again Dad said that the woods and low clouds could play havoc with acoustics. "Dad said things can sound funny sometimes," she added aloud to Ozzie.

They headed further up the field, but both seemed tenser than they had before. Clodagh could feel it in Ozzie's back, his walk was more stilted too, as if he were focused entirely on the woods. If she had felt spooked before, seeing Ozzie like this was making Clodagh feel worse.

"You think there's something there too, don't you?" she said rubbing his neck. Clodagh knew if she was tense, it would make Ozzie worse. She tried to push the thoughts of spooky ghosts from her mind and focus on something else, but it was difficult.

They were almost halfway up the field, through the nearly bare trees she could just see the brook and the ford. Once there had been a little bridge over it, but now there was just a jumble of stone and for a second, just one second, Clodagh could have sworn she saw a white/grey horse beside it. Then in a whirl of long mane and streaming tail, the image was gone. Clodagh sat frozen on Ozzie staring into the woods not sure what she had just seen.

"Did I, Ozzie, did I just see a ghost horse?" she whispered.

Ozzie snorted and pranced a little under her. Without another thought, she turned him towards the open gate that led to the top paddock and cantered towards it away from the woods. The sky seemed to grow darker with every hoofbeat, the trees behind them rustled as the wind picked up again, sending another shiver down Clodagh's spine.

By the time they reached the little metal gate that led out of the field into the cobbled yard outside the manors coach barn, big fat drops of rain had begun to fall. Clodagh slipped down from Ozzie and eyed the gate. The thought of leaving him outside in the paddock right now seemed somehow wrong. She was sure something was going on. She had seen something in the woods. Ozzie had seen it too, and now it was raining, threatening to get heavier with every second.

Mrs. Fitz appeared at the barn door. "Is everything alright dear? I saw you two cantering up the field."

Clodagh suddenly felt silly. She'd spooked herself and yet she didn't feel brave enough to admit that or to turn Ozzie loose. "Yes, it just started to rain."

Mrs. Fitz nodded. "Looks like we might get quite a downpour." She eyed Clodagh with shrewd eyes and smiled. "Maybe you should let Ozzie stay indoors tonight, pop him in. I think Dancer comes tomorrow, might be nice for him to have had a comfortable night's sleep before the excitement."

Clodagh smiled with relief and nodded. "Thanks' Mrs. Fitz, I think I will."

"You go sort him out. I was just about to make a cocoa if you'd like one?"

"Yes please," she smiled as she pulled open the gate and led Ozzie through it. Somehow, she felt better once she'd closed the little gate and taken Ozzie past the old mounting block, through the double gates, and into one of the dry, stone boxes that sat inside the manor courtyard. The rain was cascading down by the time she had grabbed Ozzie some hay and thrown down some shavings. Looking at the sky it was going to be that way for some time too. Clodagh gave Ozzie a hug and pat before heading towards the old groom's cottage Mrs. Fitz now lived in. She felt a little ashamed of herself for getting so spooked, but looking at the weather, Ozzie was going to be happy she had.

Chapter 4

Clodagh stretched as she sat up in bed. She could tell by the bright, pinkish light peeking around the edges of her curtains that it was dawn, and a nice one at that. She smiled. The night before had been very wet. By the time she had sat down with Mrs. Fitz for a cup of cocoa, it had been bucketing down so hard the window pains had been covered in a sheet of water. Mrs. Fitz had lit the fire and they'd sat around chatting about the Halloween party and how everything was going, hoping in vain that the rain would stop so Clodagh could walk home without getting soaked. In the end, though it hadn't. but luckily Dad had called up to drop off the newly arrived projector and drove her home.

She slipped out of bed and padded across to the window still half asleep. Drawing open the heavy drapes she glanced down into the paddock. A small grey shape, tucked up by the hedge close to the manor peered back and she smiled letting the curtains fall closed. It took her until she was halfway across the room to remember that she'd left Ozzie in the night before. She stopped dead in her tracks and turned back to the curtains as if a monster were hiding behind them.

Quickly she rushed back and pulled them wide apart revealing the whole window. She scanned the field, looking over every inch, but there was nothing there. She rubbed her eyes. Had she imagined the little white horse? Was she so used to seeing Ozzie there and so sleepy she'd just dreamt him up? She swallowed hard; she was sure there had been a horse in the paddock.

Hurriedly she pulled on a thick jumper and some jodhpurs, determined to find out what was going on. Pulling open her door she slipped into the corridor and darted down the stairs ready to run and grab her coat. She was almost there when Ma's voice called out from the kitchen doorway.

"Not before breakfast you don't young lady." Clodagh turned around to argue that she was just going to check something, but one look at Ma told her it was pointless. She sighed and stomped back towards the kitchen.

"Oh, and go brush your hair love," Ma said as she headed back towards the pile of toast she was buttering. "You look like Ozzie's dragged you through a hedge backward in a gale."

"Ma?" Ma glanced over at her. "Do you, do you believe in ghosts?"

Ma smiled. "I don't know," she said. "I'd like to think we all go somewhere after we leave this mortal coil, so I suppose I hope they do exist, but I've never seen one. Why do you ask?"

"Oh, just the Halloween stories, they got me thinking," Clodagh said, it wasn't really a lie.

"Well, I can tell you one thing your Great Gran used to say when we spooked ourselves with silly stories," Ma said waving the butter knife. "She'd sit us down and say the dead can't hurt you dears, only the living can do that."

Clodagh wasn't exactly sure what her Great Gran had meant by that, but it sounded oddly comforting and she smiled at Ma before heading back upstairs to find her hairbrush. She was still wondering what she had seen in the paddock a half hour later when she came back down for breakfast.

*

Ozzie pranced around at the gateway to the field as Clodagh unhooked the latch. Mike had arrived just as she was finishing her toast to help out with the Halloween decorations. He frowned as Ozzie almost dashed through the gate and spun around, his head high, ears pricked, nostrils flared.

"What's up with Ozzie?" he asked.

Clodagh almost sighed with relief that he'd asked. "I don't know, but something's going on." She undid Ozzie's headcollar and he trotted off with his nose pressed down to the ground, like some sort of scent dog on the hunt.

"What?" Mike asked curiously.

Clodagh lent on the metal gate not sure what to say. Mike was her best friend and if anyone wouldn't think she was crazy, it was him. She bit her lip a little.

"Ok, I keep seeing something, in the paddock."

"Okay," he said slowly. "Might need a bit more than that."

"A horse, ok, I keep seeing a ghost horse."

"A ghost horse." Clodagh winced, if Mike thought she was being silly then she was definitely in trouble.

"Well, I think so. Look, the other night we were telling ghost stories and I told the one about the manor,"

Mike cut her off. "The one with the girl that disappears on a horse."

Clodagh nodded. "Anyway, I went to close the windows and I thought I saw a white horse running in the trees."

Mike thought about it for a second. "But you'd just been telling stories right, so maybe you just thought you saw something."

"That's what I thought too, until yesterday. So, last night we rode around the paddock. When we were about halfway up we heard this horse whinny. Both of us, I know Ozzie heard it too." Clodagh said. "And before you say it, yes, I know Briary's not far away, but it came from the wrong direction for it to have been one of Sandra's horses. Plus Ozzie was getting all tense. Then this morning I swear I saw a grey horse in the top corner of the paddock!"

Mike rubbed his chin and gazed out over the field. Ozzie was still roaming around up by the trees in the top corner.

"Ok," he said simply. "So, ghost horse. Cool."

"You, believe me?" Clodagh said.

"Sure, I know you're not making things up and for sure Ozzie is not acting normal, so something's going on. Ghost horse is our working theory. Let's go check out the corner where Ozzie is, you said that's where you saw it right?"

Clodagh nodded. They headed across the field towards Ozzie. He happily scooted over to them and followed as they walked the fence line. There was plenty of evidence that a very real horse had been there. The grass had been flattened in places and there were hoof marks. The trouble was they could all have been made by Ozzie.

Mike sighed. "What do you know about this ghost story anyway?" he asked peering at the fence for any clues.

"Just what I told you," Clodagh replied. "Why?"

"Well, look, if there was never a lady Lilly there can't be a ghost Lilly, right?"

It was a good point and one Clodagh hadn't considered. She nodded and Mike smiled. "So, let's see if we can find any evidence that there was a Lilly. If there isn't then it's probably not a ghost horse; it's you spooking yourself and Ozzie picking up on it. You said horses do that right?"

Clodagh nodded. "But where would we find out about Lilly? I don't really want to go around admitting I think I saw a ghost horse. If Ma finds out she'll think I'm spooking myself and probably ban me from the grown-up party."

Mike smiled. "I know just the place to find out and the perfect ruse."

*

Rachel's Mum glanced up from the book she was stamping and smiled as Clodagh and Mike entered the library. It was a wonderful old building that had once been a church, some of the old pews were still huddled together in one area, surrounding a big rug so people could sit and read.

"Morning," Rachel's Mum whispered. "What are you to up then?"

"Hi, Ms. White," Mike smiled. "We were wondering if you had any old records from the manor. Or the old parish records. We were sort of hoping to do a bit of research on the old manor house that was there before, get some ideas for the party."

"What a good idea," Ms. White smiled. She looked a bit like Rachel when she did. "Let me see, I don't know much about the manor documents, but the parish records I can show you. I think Mr. Perkins will know about anything else, he's worked here forever." She checked her watch. "He'll be in about half ten. I'll show you the parish stuff and when he comes in I'll ask him."

They thanked Ms. White and followed her past the rows of bookshelves that had been erected in the old nave. At the very end, she opened a door into what had once been the chancel. It was much cosier in the little old room. A large desk with a few wheelie chairs sat in the centre and around it rows of shelving filled with boxes.

"Here we are. Now, the really old records are on the far wall, there are births, deaths, and marriages going right back to the time you're looking for, but I warn you they are hit and miss and I'm not sure how they'll help with decorations."

"Oh, it will," Mike said. "We want to know more about the family that built it, so we can get a better feel for the place. Clodagh, Beth, and Rachel had the idea to make the basement more like the old manor was back then, but with a few more spider webs and things."

"Spooky," Ms. White smiled. "Well, I'll let you get on. You'll be seeing Rachel later anyway, she's getting things ready for Dancer's move."

Ms. White turned and left them alone in the little room. Mike beamed and headed straight over to the wall she had said contained the oldest documents. He started scanning the notes written on the boxes.

"When was Lilly born?"

"I don't know," Clodagh said. Mike glanced at her. There would be a lot of records to go through if they didn't narrow things down.

"Well, when did the Fitzgeralds build the new manor?"

"Erm, about 1800 I think."

"That doesn't help much." Mike sighed.

He frowned. "Look at this."

Clodagh walked over and looked at the box Mike was pointing at. It was labelled copy old maps. He pulled it off the shelf and took it to the table, opening it up and pulling out several photocopied sheets. Spreading them out, Clodagh realised they were looking at old maps of the village and the surrounding land.

"There!" Mike pointed.

On the map was a cluster of little squares marked manor house (ruin). Clodagh smiled. There was no sign of the gatehouse she lived in, but Ozzie's field was marked on, exactly where it was today.

"What date is this?"

"1780," Mike said. "Ok, so if it was a ruin then..." He trailed off flicking through the maps. He stopped suddenly and smiled. "Bingo."

He pulled out another sheet and unfolded it. The picture was a little different, but Clodagh soon spotted what they needed. There was the manor and under it, in italicised letters were the words 'Manor (Beaushaw)'.

"We got a surname," Mike smiled.

"And a date, when is this?"

Mike squinted at the date. "1568."

Clodagh hurried over to the shelves and began reading over the titles until she found one marked 1568-1570. She pulled it out while Mike packed away the maps. Inside the box were the parish registers. They took a few volumes each and began to sift through the pages. There were several mentions of Beaushaw, but they mostly seemed to be mentioned as male deaths or marriages.

Then, turning an old page, Clodagh saw something that made her gasp. Halfway down the ledger of deaths, marked out in beautifully scrawled letters were the words Lillian Beaushaw, 1570, cause of death, unknown and beside it, squeezed onto the line 'missing'.

A cold shiver ran up Clodagh's spine. She nudged Mike and pointed with a trembling finger to the ledger. Mike looked from the book to Clodagh and back again.

"Heavy," he muttered. Whatever he was about to say next was cut short when the door opened and a balding man with a cheery face and moustache entered.

"You must be Mike and Clodagh," he smiled and Clodagh tried to smile back. "I'm Mr. Pruitt, Rosemary told me you wanted to know about the old Beaushaw place. I have something for you to look at."

He beamed as he placed a large, very old-looking book on the table in front of them. "Now, I'm not supposed to let you look at the historic records without supervision, but I really need to sort a few things and Rosemary said you are very trustworthy, so." He handed them both gloves. "I'll let you have it for fifteen minutes, ok?"

"What is it?" Mike asked.

"Oh," Mr. Pruitt put his hand on his forehead. "Silly me, I'd forget my head if it wasn't screwed on. This is the house ledger from the Beaushaw manor. Lists everything there was in the house between 1568 and 1570 when it was sold. Have fun," he said and he was gone.

Mike pulled on the gloves and began to look over the pages. He read aloud as he did and soon enough Clodagh shook the daze of seeing Lilly's name off and began to read over his shoulder. Most of the things listed seemed to be furniture or artworks, but one page began to list farm animals. Pigs, cattle, sheep, and then, at the bottom, Clodagh saw the word horses.

She began to read the section more carefully. There was a list of what type of horse, the height and purpose, and in some cases a name. Ayner, stallion, charger, chestnut. Clodagh scanned the names and then came to the bottom of the page. Carefully, her fingers trembling, she took hold of the corner, the wafer-thin, yellowed parchment threatening to give way if she turned too fast. Slowly she flipped over the paper and looked to see the horse list continued.

Three horses down was a name she recognised. Veillantif, stallion, palfrey, bay. The line had been ruled through. Clodagh pointed to the line and looked at Mike. "That's Lilly's horse.

"Holy..." Mike looked around him and made an eak face realising he was in the old church.

"They were real," Clodagh said. "Lilly and Veillantif, they were real."

Mike frowned. "Didn't you say you saw a white-grey horse?" he asked. Clodagh nodded. "It says here bay, that's brown right, like Maverick?"

Clodagh nodded. "But, would a ghost horse still be bay?"

"Good point," Mike added. "Wow, you could have actually seen a ghost."

Clodagh swallowed hard, the thought might have been exciting to Mike, but it had just made her feel more worried. She realised she had hoped to not find anything that proved Lilly could have been real.

"You know," Mike said seeing her face. "Just because Lilly was real, doesn't mean the whole story is true or that she's a ghost. Maybe it's just based on her."

That was true, Clodagh mused. There were lots of times stories were made up or embellished, perhaps Lilly's had been too. The image of the grey horse standing in the field drifted back to her and she shuddered. Then again, maybe it was real.

Chapter 5

Clodagh stepped out of the old church come library, blinking in the bright sunshine. She still wasn't exactly sure how she felt about knowing Lilly and Veillantif had been real. Mike skipped down the steps beside her and she smiled.

"Are you sure you don't want to come into town and meet up with Beth and Rachel?" she asked. "We're looking at Halloween costumes you know, not dresses."

"Thanks, but, well, I kind of agreed to go to the movies with someone," he said rubbing the toe of his sneaker on the pavement.

Clodagh grinned, "Who?"

"Ali King," he confessed, blushing as he did so. Clodagh laughed loudly. She liked Ali, but she was super girly.

"Wow, really?" Mike nodded still looking at the pavement. Clodagh couldn't help but giggle a little more at his discomfort. "Well, ok, we'll let you off this time, just promise you'll get a costume for the party." A thought occurred to her. "Are you bringing Ali?"

"What! Maybe, I don't know." He seemed more flustered by her question than by finding out that real ghost horses could be wandering around the manor. Clodagh nudged him in the arm.

"It's cool if you do you know," she said.

"Thanks," he said. "I'll call you later?"

"You better," Clodagh said as she skipped down the stone steps in the direction of town. "I want to hear all about it," she called over her shoulder.

The news that Mike had asked Ali to the pictures had taken Clodagh's mind off the idea of ghosts and she found herself walking into town feeling a little better than she had before. Maybe it was all in her head. Even if Lilly's story was based on a real girl and a real horse, it didn't mean that she had met fairies or jumped from a cliff and it didn't mean she or Veillantif haunted the manor one week a year. In fact, as she drew closer to the shops, Clodagh convinced herself she must have been imagining things because up until she had heard the story from Mrs. Fitz, she had never seen anything spooky at either the manor or the B&B.

"Hey," Clodagh looked over to see Beth and Rachel standing by the old war monument in the centre of town. She waved at them and hurried over.

"You are never going to believe my day," she said.

"Tell us as we go," Beth said, ushering them towards the shops. "We have two hours to find costumes or we'll all be cutting holes in dust sheets."

Everyone laughed, but let Beth herd them towards the closest shop. The shops in town were few and far between. Other than the supermarket and the charity shop, their costume options were limited to Carter's Hardware and Goods and Mrs. Milligan's tea rooms. They all agreed Mrs. Mulligans had fantastic cakes but would be useless for finding something spooky to wear to a party and so they started in Mr. Carter's.

Clodagh began to explain all about how she and Mike had been researching the manor, leaving out the part about the ghost horse. She didn't really want to remind herself of it now that she had decided the whole thing was in her imagination. The fact that Lilly had been a real person though was a very cool detail to add to the Halloween party and both Beth and Rachel agreed it had to be worked in somehow. The fact Mike had gone to the pictures with Ali King though caused almost more consternation. Rachel especially demanded details that Clodagh couldn't give her.

"Ali King," she repeated as they wandered inside the Hardware store. "Really? She's so, so..."

"Girly?" Clodagh suggested.

"Yeah," Rachel nodded. "I mean, nice, but..."

"Pink," Beth added with a smile.

"Hey, I like pink!" Rachel objected. Beth giggled.

Clodagh turned her head so Rachel couldn't see her giggle too and concentrated on the displays around her. Carter's always amazed Clodagh. It was an Aladdin's cave of things. Paint and nails sat on an aisle opposite cake tins and piles of Pyrex dishes. There were gardening supplies, some lights, a whole array of cheaply priced toys for children, stationery, and other assorted homewares all packed tightly together. Old Mr. Carter always sat behind a wooden desk at the back of the shop reading a paper with his glasses halfway down his nose. As usual, when his shop bell dinged, he glanced up, waved, and smiled before going back to the crossword.

The shop also had one corner dedicated to seasonal supplies. In the winter this meant a stack of rock salt, Christmas decorations, and wreaths, and spring saw bulbs and seeds. In autumn though it was all about Halloween. They hustled over to the corner. A metal stand full of stickers showing pumpkins and bats, paper garlands, and balloons was stood next to the main shelves. Clodagh looked over at them, a series of battery-light pumpkins, and a cat looked back at her from beside an array of plastic masks that were held on by elastic. She wrinkled her nose.

"I'm not sure these are what we're looking for," she said a little sadly.

Beth picked up a werewolf mask and shook her head. "Nope."

"Should we try the charity next door?" Rachel suggested. "We could maybe put something together."

"Come on then."

They waved bye to Mr. Carter and headed into the charity shop next door. Here there was a Halloween theme, with crepe paper cut outs in the windows, but despite looking around they couldn't find anything that would work for Halloween.

The last option was the supermarket. It was a local one but did have a few Halloween costumes hanging up on a rail next to a huge pallet of pumpkins. They began to go through them. Pirates, skeletons, and witches seemed to make up the options, none of which seemed quite right. Clodagh sighed.

"Maybe we should try online," she suggested.

"Well, I'm not," Beth said. "I swore if I didn't find anything here, I was going to borrow something off Sarah. She went to two Halloween parties last year at university and offered to let me pinch a costume. I sort of wanted my own, but..."

"Which costumes did she have?" Rachel asked.

"Zombie student and a witch. I think I'll go witch. I did think about going in my show gear as a dead eventer, but Dad said it wouldn't work unless I took Mav."

"I could just see you putting chalk all over Maverick to make him a ghost horse," Rachel laughed.

Her words made Clodagh think back to Lilly and for a second, she felt a knot form in her stomach again, but she shook it away, concentrating on the costume issue.

"Well, I'm off to hunt on the internet," Rachel said. "What about you Clodagh, what are you going to do?"

"I'm not sure," she replied honestly. "Maybe I'll look online too, I still have a day or two." She glanced at her watch. "We better go. Ma said she'd pick me up in five minutes. Are you bringing Dancer over tonight?"

Rachel nodded. "Grandad said he'd sort out the trailer while I was here. Do you think it would be ok to leave my tack with yours? That way I can ride after school sometimes and maybe bike home."

Clodagh nodded. "There's tons of space. Dad even has the old racks from the manor tack room stored in the garage, I'll see if he'll put one up on the wall under my rack."

"Thanks," Rachel smiled.

Beth's phone made a pinging noise and she pulled it out of her pocket and smiled. "It's Melissa. She says she and Ash are heading to the airport in an hour." She smiled. "She wants to know what our costumes are." Beth started typing a reply.

"What are you saying?" Rachel asked.

"I'm sorted, Rachel's surfing the net and Clodagh's so busy she's wearing a sheet with eye holes, possibly she'll cover Ozzie in one and go as Lady Lilly." Rachel laughed, but Clodagh gently slapped her arm.

"Hey!" Beth's phone pinged again and she turned it around to show three laughing faces. Clodagh huffed a little but smiled when Beth put her arm around her.

They headed out of the shops and split off going their separate ways. Clodagh wandered back to the monument and sat on the side of it waiting for Ma.

*

Rachel and Dancer arrived at the manor later in the afternoon. They had decided that the best thing to do was to move Ozzie back to the bottom paddock and let Dancer have the top for a few days before opening the gate in the middle and letting them graze together. Ozzie was already at the middle gate when Dancer came off the trailer and whinnied. Rachel smiled.

"Welcome to your new home," She said and Dancer looked at her curiously.

"Well, not exactly new." Mrs. Fitz smiled. "Been here before haven't you Missy." She patted Dancer's neck.

The mare gave a little snort and tossed her head. Mel finished pushing up the trailer ramp and dusted his hands on his trousers.

"Can't thank you enough for letting her come to stay," he said.

"It's quite alright." Mrs. Fitz replied. "I do like having horses around the place. Feels right."

"Come on," Clodagh said. "Let's go pop her out."

She and Rachel walked towards the big gate at the side of the top paddock. It hadn't been used in a while, since Clodagh almost always used the little metal wicket gate, so when they swung it open the hinges creaked.

"You want to tape that sound for your Halloween party," Mel said with a smile.

Dancer walked through the gate looking around herself. She was pretty used to the manor and its fields, but seemed to sense this time was different. Rachel undid her head collar and she trotted off into the field. Ozzie spotted her and shouted loudly. She stopped and lifted her head looking at him before shouting back and hurtling across the field towards him. She bounced to a stop by the gate and they sniffed at each other over the fence, their noses touching.

"Aww," Rachel said.

Clodagh smiled. She loved Ozzie more than anything or anyone in the whole world, but she often wondered if he got a little lonely when she wasn't around. Did he feel bored when she was at school with no one to talk to or play with? Now he had a friend for when she wasn't there. It made her smile. Something caught Dancer's attention and her head flashed over towards the woods. Clodagh felt her heart race, but when she looked over, she didn't see a thing and

Dancer quickly turned her attention back to Ozzie. It's just in my mind, Clodagh told herself, it's not a ghost.

"Would you all like a cup of tea?" Mrs. Fitz asked.

"Only if it's no trouble," Mel replied.

"None at all, actually I was hoping you might help me out. Farmer Bob is bringing by a load of pumpkins in fifteen minutes. I rather think I could use some young hands to move them," Mrs. Fitz smiled.

"We'll help," Clodagh offered, glancing at Rachel.

"Me too, least I can do," Mel added as they followed Mrs. Fitz through the coaching barn door towards the cottage.

They passed the magnificent old gig that Mrs. Fitz still owned and climbed a short flight of stairs into the passage that ran past Mrs. Fitz's front door. Mrs. Fitz had just pushed the door open when the phone began to ring. She ushered them into the kitchen and hurried into the little living room, picking up the receiver. She put her hand over the mouthpiece and glanced back their way.

"Pop the kettle on please Clodagh, you know where the mugs are."

Clodagh smiled and picked the little on the hob kettle up from the black stove top, filling it at the large Belfast sink she put it back and flicked on the gas. Rachel was looking out of the window over the paddock beyond. Dancer was still stood happily grazing with Ozzie on the other side of the fence. She nudged her Grandad and he smiled.

"Oh, no, really!" they heard Mrs. Fitz saying. "Well, you'll let me know if I can help Angela." There were a few moments of silence. "Yes, yes I will."

Mrs. Fitz came back into the kitchen looking a little sad. Mel frowned; he cleared his throat. "Everything alright Mrs. Fitz?"

"Oh, no, not really. That was Angela, her stallion broke loose and is missing from the stud. I'd been wondering why I couldn't get hold of her. I'd hope she'd come and drive the gig with her two big lads, I suppose that's not going to happen now."

Clodagh's heart sank. She had met Angela's stallion, Zeus; he was the grandson of Mrs. Fitz's old driving horse, Achilles. She hoped Angela could find him quickly. Clodagh opened her mouth to suggest that they go and help search for him when there was a loud ringing noise from the front gates.

"Oh, that'll be Farmer Bob." They all hustled out of the cottage following Mrs. Fitz down to the gates.

Sure enough, when they got there, Farmer Bob was there waiting with a huge box of pumpkins.

"These should keep you going," he said with a smile.

"Not caving them all are you?" Mel asked, eyeing up the pile of orange.

"Well, maybe not," She looked over at Clodagh and Rachel. "I think I'd like to nip over and check on Angela, make sure she's alright. Do you think you two girls could sort this lot out, pick the best four or five to carve?"

Clodagh nodded. She'd have rather gone to Angela's too, but she knew this is what she needed to do right now, besides they really ought to keep an eye on Ozzie and Dancer for just a little longer.

"Can take you over if you like," Mel offered. "Might be a useful second pair of eyes and the trailers already on if we spot him on route."

"Thank you very much," Mrs. Fitz smiled.

She and Mel went to the car and stepped inside, while Clodagh and Rachel began to scoop up the pumpkins. Mrs. Fitz wound down her window and popped her head out for a second.

"Left the door open girls and the connecting one to the manor, would you mind awfully letting Pip out for a few minutes and locking up if I'm not back when you're done?"

"Of course," Clodagh said. "Please tell Angela we hope she finds Zeus." She called, but her last few words were lost to the sound of Mel's old truck engine roaring into life.

"Come on," Farmer Bob smiled. "I'll help you shift and sort this lot. I haven't carved a pumpkin yet this year."

Clodagh smiled and adjusted the huge pumpkin in her arms. "Maybe we should carve the smaller ones?"

"Nah," Rachel smiled. "Let's do the huge ones. They'll be spookier."

They headed back towards the cottage. As they passed through the kitchen, Clodagh looked up and saw both ponies watching something in the woods. She shook her head, it was nothing, just a bird or something they saw. It's not a ghost. It's not a ghost, she repeated in her head, but as much as she willed herself to believe it, a small part of her just wasn't certain.

She trusted Ozzie completely and she realised that was why she couldn't shake the feeling something was odd. Ozzie was telling her she wasn't crazy. Maybe there really was a ghost horse.

Chapter 6

Ozzie pulled up a mouthful of grass and munched on it happily as he looked over the fence at Dancer. Clodagh smiled, the little black pony hadn't so much as lifted her head the whole time she had been sitting in the paddock. It was surprisingly mild considering Halloween was only two days away. Two days. Clodagh sighed, there was still so much to do. The manor was pretty much decorated and Ma was handling the food, but there was still the pumpkin ride trail to set up and she still had nothing to wear to the party. She tapped the pencil in her hand on the notebook laid on the picnic rug she was sitting on.

Mrs. Fitz had asked her to work out the route the pumpkin hack would take and what sort of things they could put on it. She knew that going through the woods would be fun, but it would be getting dark. Maybe if they did that section first, she mused, but then they'd have to ride down the manor drive.

"Working hard?" Dad asked as he leaned over the fence behind her.

Clodagh sighed. "I can't work out how to do the pumpkin ride without having to go back on ourselves," she said. "I guess we could come down the drive, but then we'd have to ride through the manor gardens. I know Mrs. Fitz doesn't mind me and Ozzie nipping through, but this is different."

"What you need," Dad said looking thoughtful, "is a bridge over the brook."

"That'd help," Clodagh chuckled. "Then we could ride back through the gate and over the road to the big gate at Briary. Shame it wasn't safe and collapsed. Though I suppose we could ride through the stream, but there's going to be a few people walking with the ride, they'd get their feet wet."

Dad smiled. "Not anymore. I fixed up a wooden bridge over the stream, it's not for horses, but it'll take a person walking and a dog. Basil and I tried it out."

"Really!" Clodagh exclaimed. "Why didn't you say something?"

"I figured you and Ozzie would know, you ride there all the time," Dad frowned.

Clodagh fiddled with her pencil. "We haven't been that way for a while," She admitted, wondering how much she should tell Dad. "Things have been so busy."

"Well, go check it out. You should ride the route you've chosen, then you can work out what decorations you want to put where. Best do it today, we won't have long to set it up."

Clodagh scrambled up to her feet. "I'll do it now."

Dad looked at his watch. "Don't be too long mind, your friends are coming this afternoon aren't they?"

Clodagh nodded. She scooped up the picnic rug and folded it up before clambering over the fence and walking with Dad back towards the gatehouse. She looked over her shoulder as they walked.

"Back in a minute Ozzie," she called. He snorted at her and cropped another bit of grass.

*

Clodagh decided to start her test run at the manor drive gates. She checked her watch and made a note of the time.

"Right Ozzie, here we go," she urged Ozzie into a walk along the track that ran along the bottom of his field. "Let's hope we don't run into fairies."

Entering the woods, Clodagh felt a little tense, but she shook it off. This was the woods, her and Ozzie's woods, they knew them better than anyone. It was their safe place. They followed the trail, Ozzie plodding along as usual. The trees had lost their leaves now and would look great on the pumpkin ride. Maybe it would be a little dark though, she mused. There were lots of solar fairy lights in the garage though and with some lanterns hung in the trees. That might work.

The trail slowly started to slope upwards and Clodagh found herself relaxing with every step they took. Focusing on the trail and the decoration ideas was really helping. She saw a few places where they could put pumpkins and station helpers. They reached the fork in the track and turned down to the stream. Sure enough, a lovely little wooden arched bridge had been secured over the brook. It was low and narrow, with wooden handrails, perfect for any helpers to cross.

Clodagh was just wondering if they could put some lights here too when a flash of white appeared in her peripheral vision and Ozzie turned his head sharply. Clodagh instinctively tightened her hands on Ozzie's reins as she turned to see what it was. Something white was moving swiftly through the trees on the opposite side of the brook, high up the hill towards the forty acres.

"Let's check it out," Clodagh said suddenly sick of being scared. She and Ozzie splashed through the stream and cantered up the bank into the forty acres. She had been sure whatever she had seen was heading this way too, but when they reached the big open field, it was empty. Turning Ozzie, she trotted along the edge of the field looking down into the woods as they went, trying to spot something. Nothing.

"Where'd it go?" she asked Ozzie, he just snorted and tossed his head.

Clodagh felt her heart pounding. Had she really seen the phantom horse again? Ozzie jiggled his reins, getting her attention. She glanced into the woods wanting to look more, she glanced at her watch, they were off schedule and still had the rest of the trail to check. Reluctantly she turned Ozzie around and headed back down the field, still scanning the woods.

They reached the gate to the road and Clodagh opened it, making a note that there would need to be someone to man it. She was closing the latch when she heard the sound of cantering hooves and there, at the very far side of the field, just for a second, she was sure she saw a white/grey horse emerge from the tree line before it dipped back into the woods. Clodagh swallowed hard and turned Ozzie quickly back towards Briary.

There was no doubt in her mind she had seen a horse. Her hands shaking, Clodagh unlatched the gate on the Briary side of the road and headed along the last bit of the loop.

"You saw it too, right Ozzie?" she said. He tossed his head. As they rode Clodagh tried to calm down. Perhaps it hadn't been a horse. It could have been a white bag of something snagged in one of the trees, blowing out for a second, but deep down she didn't buy her own lie.

When she reached Briary she saw one of Sandra's girls standing leaning on the gate. The girl waved as Clodagh rode up.

"Hey, you didn't see Charlotte while you were out, did you?" the girl asked.

Clodagh frowned. "No, why?"

"She's late, she said she was only going out for half an hour and that was forty-five minutes ago."

"Really? You want me to go look for her?" Clodagh offered.

"No, never mind, look." Clodagh looked back to see Charlotte and Gracie opening the gate they had come through a few minutes before. Clodagh sighed with relief, Gracie was large and white/grey.

"Thanks for offering to help," the girl smiled. "We're all looking forward to your trail ride by the way."

"Thanks," Clodagh smiled. "I better get going, I'm late."

She turned Ozzie for home, trotting off up the lane and waving to Charlotte as they went.

"I bet we saw Gracie," Clodagh sighed to Ozzie. "She was late, she probably cut through the woods to get back before dark. I have to stop spooking myself, don't I." She chuckled as they reached the road and headed back to the paddock.

*

Clodagh had just pulled Ozzie's bridle off over his neat little grey ears when a strange car pulled up the driveway and stopped outside the B&B. She watched with curiosity as the back doors opened and Melissa leapt out, her blond hair bouncing as she went. Ash stepped out of the other side and waved. A few seconds later and they were rushing over towards her as she climbed over the gate and they fell into a three-way hug.

Ozzie, eager to join in the reunion, began to nudge them all and Melissa laughed, pulling out of the hug to fuss him, rubbing his neck as he nuzzled her pockets.

"Good to see you too Ozzie," she smiled.

"Yeah," Ash added, patting his neck. "It feels like forever!"

"How are the plans going?" Melissa asked excitedly, her eyes dancing. "Is it epic, oh, no don't tell me I want to be surprised. No, no, tell me I can't wait!"

"She's been like this the whole trip." Ash sighed smiling at Clodagh. His sister slapped his arm.

"Why don't we get your things and settle in, then if you want I'll tell you all about it," Clodagh said.

"Great!" Melissa said. She skipped off back towards the car where a driver had begun to unload a lot of bags from the boot.

Clodagh picked up her grooming bag and bridle, giving Ozzie a pat before reaching for her saddle.

"I'll get it," Ash said, scooping it up. "Say, isn't that Dancer?"

Clodagh nodded. "Mel's retiring."

"Oh," Ash said. "How's that going?"

"Well, it's not too bad," Clodagh said honestly. "I'll let Rachel catch you up on her plans, they're pretty cool."

"And what about the manor, how are things here?"

Clodagh thought about it for a second. She sighed. "The manor is doing great. Letting it out after the film has really turned the place around."

"But?" Ash said, eyeing her.

Clodagh bit her lip wondering if she should tell him about the phantom horse or not. "There's been some stuff happening. Maybe. Possibly?" she tried.

"Stuff?"

Clodagh took a deep breath. "I'm not sure if you'd believe me if I told you."

"Try me," he said.

"I think there may be a phantom horse hanging around Ozzie's paddock," she said flatly.

Ash stopped and turned to look at her as if trying to decide if she were teasing him. He shook his head. "I think you might need to explain that one a bit."

They reached the car and Clodagh looked over the pile of luggage sitting in the driveway.

"That one's mine," Ash said pointing with his toe to a single black suitcase. "The rest are Mel's."

Melissa huffed and crossed her arms over her chest. "That's not true!" she said and then added quietly. "The little black one is yours too."

Ash laughed. "I'll go get Sam and Dad to help move these." Clodagh smiled and then stopped. She looked back at Ash. "Don't tell them what I said about the phantom. They don't know and I think if Ma finds out she'll stop me going to the party."

Melissa looked at Ash in confusion, but he nodded his head. Clodagh took her saddle off him and headed into the house to find a few more pairs of hands.

*

"So, you really saw it, a ghost horse in the field," Melissa asked.

They were sat in Clodagh's room together, Ash on her desk chair, Melissa and Clodagh on the bed. She nodded,

"But, I mean, a ghost horse?" Ash asked.

"You remember the story I told you. The ghost story from the manor?" Clodagh asked. Ash nodded. "Well, me and Mike went down to the library and dug through the old registers. There really was a Lady Lilly at the manor. I'd say it was in my head, or that it was some odd coincidence, but it's Halloween week and well, Ozzie saw it too. I swear he did."

Melissa glanced over at Ash and back to Clodagh. Clodagh pulled her pillow off the bed and hugged it to her. She hoped that Ash and Melissa didn't think she was some silly girl getting too into Halloween.

"Well, I'm not sure I buy a ghost horse haunting the field," Ash started; Clodagh felt her heart sink. "But, if Ozzie is acting strange and seeing what you are, there must be something." Clodagh looked up and smiled, at least he believed she'd seen something.

Melissa tilted her head a little. "You said you saw a horse." Clodagh nodded. "But, in the story the horse and the girl, Lilly, they're together all the time. Really close right." Clodagh nodded again. "So, why would you only see the horse?"

It was a great question and one Clodagh hadn't thought about before. She'd always just assumed the horse was Veillantif, but Melissa had a point, why was she only seeing the horse and not the rider?

"I don't know," Clodagh said honestly.

"Well, we better keep our eyes open," Ash said.

"Say, changing the subject, is there anywhere close by where I could get some ribbon?" Melissa asked.

"Ma might have some, what's it for?"

Melissa smiled. "Wings, I need a bit of sheer ribbon to finish them off for my costume."

"There's a haberdashery place in the big town," Clodagh said.

"Perfect." Melissa smiled.

A sudden thought crossed Clodagh's mind. She still didn't have a costume, but there would be plenty of places there to try and find one.

"Ma's going there on Halloween to pick up a cake. If you don't mind waiting I'm sure she'd give you a ride and maybe, if it's alright with you I could tag along. I still don't actually have a costume."

"Sure, I'd love the company." Melissa smiled, glancing at Ash. "We can go before the pumpkin ride."

"Oh, that reminds me, I spoke to Sandra, she said you could take one of the school horses on the ride." Clodagh smiled. Melissa clapped her hands in glee.

"Oohh, this is going to be so much fun. Did you persuade anyone to dress up in the end, you know as Lilly and Oberon?" Melissa asked.

Clodagh shook her head. "Nope, but it should be great fun anyway. I think the pumpkin ride will be amazing. I rode the trail today and worked out where to put everything. Do you want to see my ideas?"

"Sure!" Melissa smiled.

"Me too," Ash said. "But not right now, I have a couple of calls to make. You two go ahead, I'll get this done and be back soon."

He stood and headed for the door, while Clodagh went to her desk to get her notebook so she could show Melissa what she had so far. Flopping back onto the bed, she flipped through her notes. Melissa frowned as she landed on a page with scribbled notes on it under the word costume.

"What's that?" she asked.

Clodagh looked down at the notebook. "Well, I wasn't sure I'd find a costume, so I sort of made a note of what I had laying around I could use to cobble one together."

Melissa raised an eyebrow at the list. "Your school skirt?"

"It is black," Clodagh pointed out.

"We'll find something," Melissa said with a smile. "I promise, you shall go to the ball." They laughed and Melissa hugged her shoulders. "While Ash isn't here, can you tell me the ghost story again?" Clodagh smiled.

Chapter 7

Clodagh scooped pumpkin goop out of the orange fruit in front of her and dropped it with a plop into a carrier bag on the table. She looked up and smiled. Ash was trying to pull some of the seeds out with his hands, while Melissa kept saying 'ew' as she tried to lift out the slippery centre with a spoon. Rachel had picked a smaller pumpkin and was already trying to mark out a pattern on it using a felt tip marker, while Beth and Sam tackled one together.

She'd managed to get up before everyone else that morning and snuck in a quick ride with Ozzie. She had been very pleased not to see any phantom horses in the paddock when she'd arrived and apart from Dancer getting a little over-excited on the other side of the fence when they did a few canter circles, there had been nothing to really report. Ozzie seemed his usual self and Clodagh had begun to relax.

"Do these really need to be carved?" Sam asked, bringing Clodagh back to the moment.

She smiled. "Yep, come on, there's only ten of them."

Sam sighed. "Where are they going again?"

"Two at the start of the trail, two at the end, and the others dotted along the route," Clodagh replied.

"We already did the ones for the manor," Rachel added.

"Fine," Sam huffed. "I wish I'd offered to help Dad string the lights."

Clodagh smiled and shook her head. It was the day before the party and everyone was rushing around getting everything sorted so it was perfect. Dad was organising strings of solar lights they were going to put up along the pumpkin trail route, as well as some spooky decorations to hang up outside the manor itself. Ma had gone to the village for supplies and they were on carving duty, at least for now.

"Don't worry," Beth said putting her hand on Sam's arm. "I ran into your Dad as I came in, there are so many decorations to put up outside the manor I suspect we'll all have a chance to string lights." Sam rolled his eyes.

"Well, I love it." Ash beamed. "A proper Halloween, pumpkins, candy..." he sighed dreamily. "Even a party."

"Oh yes, so much better being in the damp and cold than sitting on a sandy beach in the sun surrounded by swaying palm trees listening to the sound of the sea." Rachel giggled.

"It's not the same," Melissa said. "Ash is right, as much as I don't like pumpkin goop, it is nice to be somewhere that feels like it's well, Halloween. Same at Christmas."

"You didn't spend Christmas at home?" Rachel asked.

They shook their heads. "Last year we were in Australia. It was nice, being warm and sitting around the pool, but Christmas day, I don't know, I missed the cold."

"And the snow," Ash added. "Though it was sort of cool BBQ'ing the turkey."

"It was nice last year," Beth said with a smile. "We had enough snow to go sledging."

"You did a turkey on a BBQ?" Sam asked.

Ash nodded. "It was so odd, I asked a few friends we made over there and they said it would be strange if Christmas was cold and wet. I guess Christmas is what you grow up with and Halloween is the same."

"Well, I hope we get a little bit less of normal Halloween weather and a little warmer and drier," Beth said. "At least while we ride the trail, no one wants to do a pumpkin ride in the rain."

"It's supposed to be ok," Rachel said as she finished marking her design and picked up a little saw to start cutting out the face she'd made. "Grandad checks the weather like five times a day. So far it's looking dry, maybe a little chilly though."

"I'll take it," Beth said.

The back door opened and Dad appeared holding up a fake plastic cage with an equally fake and plastic pirate skeleton inside it. He chuckled as he waved it a bit.

"Thought I'd check how it was going in here before I went and hung Charlie here up by the manor gates," he said.

"Getting there," Clodagh said holding up her pumpkin.

"Great! Look, I think I'm going to need a few hands if you can spare them later," he said. "There's a lot more than I thought."

"Sure, thing Dad," Clodagh said.

"Perfect, I'll see you all up at the manor in a bit then." He waved Charlie's hand at them and disappeared out of the door. Everyone giggled.

"Well, I guess we get to see the manor before the party after all," Melissa squealed, throwing her arms up. The spoon shot out of the pumpkin, shooting a few stringy bits and seeds over Ash. He glared at his sister who tried for a couple of seconds not to laugh before they all burst out in fits of giggles.

*

An hour later Clodagh found herself at the top of one of Dad's ladders hanging up a fake Ghost from the frame of the manor's door. It was a tangle of material with a spooky face on it. Up close it looked a little bit odd, but Clodagh guessed in the dusky light it would be alright. Dad had put Charlie and his matching friends on either side of the big green gates, while Sam had set up two fake fire baskets beneath them, complete with glowing coals. Originally, they'd thought about having real ones, but Mrs. Fitz had been less than keen on the idea after the fire. Still, even with fake embers, it looked amazing in the daylight and Clodagh could well imagine it would only look better at night.

"Where is this going?" Ash asked. Clodagh glanced down. He and Melissa had a large bundle of black and orange bunting in their arms.

"Oh, it's being zig-zagged between the stables and the garages," Clodagh said pointing. "From the gates up to the courtyard."

"On it," Melissa said.

"Clodagh," Dad called from the gateway. Clodagh looked over as she climbed down the steps. "It's getting on a bit and we need to get the pumpkin trail set up yet. I think we'd best divide and conquer."

"Ok Dad, what do you want me to do?" she asked, dusting her hands on the back of her jeans.

Dad looked around as if he was thinking. He rubbed his chin. "Well, you know the trail best, I say you take a couple of helpers and make a start on the woods, we'll finish here and then catch up with you to sort out the bit around Briary."

Clodagh nodded. "Who's coming with me?" She called, knowing everyone would have heard.

"I will," Ash called.

"Me too," Clodagh looked up to see Mike waving from the gates. "Sorry I'm late, my bike got a flat."

"I'll come too," Rachel said. "I know Melissa really wants to see inside."

"Thank you," Melissa mouthed to her as she struggled to take all the bunting from Ash.

"Brilliant," Dad smiled. "The lights are in bundles by the gatehouse, in the wheelbarrow."

Clodagh and her group headed back towards the gatehouse, cutting through the paddocks so they could say hi to Ozzie and Dancer as they went. The two ponies were still separated by the fence, but most of the time grazed together on either side.

"When are they going in together?" Mike asked patting Dancer.

"Probably after the party," Clodagh said as Ozzie nuzzled at her, ruffling his nose through her hair. "Ozzie," she giggled. "Come on, we'd better get this done before it gets dark."

"Yeah," Mike said. He wiggled his fingers a little. "And it gets spooky."

Clodagh nudged him in the arm and clambered over the fence, followed by the others. They headed over to Ozzie's paddock and picked up the wheelbarrow of lights before heading towards the woods. Ozzie, who had followed them all the way to the gate, jogged alongside them snorting at the barrow, his ears flicking in its direction.

"I think he wants to help," Mike laughed.

"Maybe he should," Ash said, struggling to keep the wheelbarrow going on the rough track. "It'd be easier to have him carry these than use this thing."

"I think the wheel's a bit flat," Rachel pointed out.

"Where should we start?" Mike asked.

"I think we should string them all along the woodland bit of the trail, it might be darker there, they won't work here," Clodagh mused.

"Ok, look how about me and Rachel start at this end and you and Ash start at the forty acres, we can meet in the middle," Mike suggested.

"Ok. We'll drop off boxes of lights as we go," Clodagh added. "It'll make the barrow easier to handle."

She and Ash began to walk further into the woods, dropping off boxes of lights every few metres. Ozzie was still shadowing them in his paddock and between him and Ash, Clodagh didn't feel spooked at all. She suddenly felt silly again but pushed the thought away as they turned towards the brook and the new bridge came into view.

"Wow," Ash said with a smile. "It looks a lot better than the last time I was here."

Clodagh nodded. "I'll never forget when it collapsed."

"Neither will I," Ash said. "I doubt Nick will either."

Clodagh thought back to the day she had watched the actor Nicholas Padget ride over the old bridge on the horse he was riding. It had been for a shot in a movie being filmed at the manor. Ash and Melissa had both starred in it too, but Nicholas had been the biggest name in the film. It had been terrifying to watch the stone bridge collapse beneath him and Troy. He'd been lucky to escape unharmed and in a way Troy had been lucky too. Although he had been injured, it hadn't been too bad and he had found a new home with Angela at the stud. The thought of Angela reminded Clodagh of Zeus. She wondered if Angela had gotten him back yet after he had escaped. Zeus and Troy could have been brothers, both large and black with thick white stripes. Zeus had even played the part Troy was supposed to in the film.

Clodagh followed Ash across the bridge and began to take the lights from the last box. Ash began hanging the little strip of orange lights in the trees while Clodagh made sure that the solar panel was in a patch of light.

"Do you still speak to Nick?" Clodagh asked, her mind still on the day the bridge had given out.

"Yeah, actually, I spoke to him yesterday. He's doing a Shakespeare play in London at the moment, they're just finishing rehearsals."

"Really? Which play?" Clodagh asked. She enjoyed doing Shakespeare at school, though they hadn't done many of them yet. Sam had some on DVD because he said it was easier to understand them if you watched the play rather than just read them. She'd watched a couple of them with him occasionally when he'd had to write English papers.

"A Midsummer Night's Dream," Ash said.

"Really? That's my favourite, we did it at school last year and Sam showed me a film version of it, only I think they used bikes and in the play, they didn't," Clodagh said.

"It's my favourite too!" Ash said. "I love the bit where they turn the guy into a donkey and Titania falls in love with him."

Clodagh giggled. "That's funny."

Clodagh wrapped the lights around the end of the bridge and stopped. She was staring so intently at the edge of the brook that Ash wandered over and looked down too.

"What is it?" he asked.

"Hoofprints." Clodagh pointed down at a set of neat little hoofprints in the mud at the side of the brook.

"What about them?" Ash asked. "Aren't they Ozzie's, they look about his size."

"They do," Clodagh frowned. "But, I thought..." She trailed off for a second then shook her head. "I must have been mistaken."

"Mistaken about what?" Ash asked. "I don't follow."

"Oh, nothing, it's just I thought Ozzie and I had ridden down the other side of the bridge the last time we were here. I was sure," Clodagh said, glancing back at the hoofprints.

"Maybe they belong to the phantom horse," Ash said with a grin.

"I don't think phantom horses leave hoofprints," Clodagh said.

"Then maybe what you've been seeing isn't a phantom," Ash suggested.

"Hey, hurry up you guys," Mike called. "We're almost done."

"I think we'd better finish up," Ash said. "But let's keep an eye out for that phantom horse of yours, I'm starting to get the feeling there's more to it than just an old ghost story."

Clodagh nodded. "We should tell the others too, but let's keep it between us for now. I'm still not sure I want to tell Dad and Ma just yet."

"You sure?" Ash asked. Clodagh thought for a second and then nodded. "Ok then." He smiled.

Chapter 8

Clodagh rushed to the window as soon as she woke up, pulling back the heavy curtains and staring at the sky. It looked like a chilly and grey October morning, but as forecast, so far, it was dry. She let out a sigh of relief and looked over at Ozzie and Dancer grazing. At least we should get to do the pumpkin ride, she thought, smiling.

"Happy Halloween!" Melissa said bursting through her bedroom door. Clodagh jumped in shock and spun around giggling when she realised who it was.

"You scared me," Clodagh laughed.

"It's Halloween, sort of the point," Melissa said. "Eak, I'm so excited. Do you know what sort of costume you want to look for this morning?"

Clodagh shook her head. She really hadn't thought much about costumes, she had been too focused on the phantom horse and party setup. Now though she only had a few hours left before the events would start and she still had nothing to wear other than her old witches hat.

"Well, we'll find something," Melissa said coming over and wrapping her arm around Clodagh's shoulders. "Something awesome."

"Mel," Ash walked up to the door rubbing his eyes. "It's like 7 am, did you wake Clodagh up?"

"No, she was up already, I heard her pottering around," Melissa said.

"It's true," Clodagh said. "I wanted to check the weather."

"It's pretty grey," Ash said running a hand through his unbrushed hair. "You think it'll be ok for later?"

"I think so, the forecast said low cloud but dry," Clodagh gestured to the window. "It's accurate so far."

"So, what's the plan?" he asked, stretching. "Please tell me it either involves more sleep or food?"

"We," Melissa hugged Clodagh, "are going shopping to find a costume."

Ash opened his mouth to say something when Ma's voice called from downstairs. "Best come on down you lot, I'll make breakfast now if you're all up."

"Come on," Clodagh said with a huge grin. "You don't want to miss Ma's Halloween breakfast! It's amazing!"

She bounded out of the room and along the landing with Ash and Melissa following behind her.

"Halloween breakfast?" she heard Ash ask and she smiled.

Ma's annual Halloween breakfast was a legend in Clodagh's house. She made pancakes in the shape of Jack O'Lanterns with chocolate eyes and a mouth, there was ghost toast with butter and special warm spiced apple juice to drink. Neither Ash nor Melissa had ever seen it before and she was eager to share the tradition with them.

When they arrived downstairs Ma was just spooning out pancake batter and seeing how much effort she had gone to, both Ash and Melissa rushed off to wash and get dressed. While they did so and Ma put the finishing touches to breakfast, Clodagh slipped out of the house and headed over to the paddock with a few carrots for Ozzie. He trotted over as soon as he spotted her and eagerly munched through the first carrot before nudging her for another. She giggled and pulled one out of her coat pocket for him.

"Any sign of our ghost horse?" she asked him. He snorted at her and took another bite. "I'll take that as a no."

Clodagh was starting to think that Ash had been right. Maybe there had been a loose horse that somehow she hadn't heard about. She hadn't seen the grey for a couple of days, it would make sense if it had been an escaped pony that had maybe been caught and taken back home. Still, it would be awfully strange. The stud was a fair few miles away and she'd heard about Zeus getting loose. Besides, if someone found a pony close to the manor, surely it would have been brought to Mrs. Fitz until an owner could collect it. Clodagh frowned as she rubbed Ozzie's neck and passed him the last carrot, it was all a little confusing, she just couldn't decide if she was looking at a real loose horse or a ghost horse from the manor's past. Neither seemed to make total sense.

The ghost story said that Lilly and her mount were free for one week a year, around the time of Halloween, to seek her true love. If the story were true then unless Lilly had somehow miraculously met up with her true love after a few hundred years that week, then she should still be wandering around the manor.

"I wonder though," Clodagh mused looking at Ozzie. "She wouldn't just check the manor right? I mean, if it was me I'd check here, but then I'd go to their meeting place."

The meeting place had been vague in the story. Mrs. Fitz had said it was out by the old McDonald place somewhere. She wondered if they should go down there and take a look, then she shook her head, if they did that, she'd never have time to find a costume. Then again, what if Lilly was there? Clodagh wondered what it would be like for her, waiting for hundreds of years and never being reunited with her true love. Clodagh sighed. Trying to figure the puzzle out was making her head hurt.

"Everything alright?" Clodagh spun around to see Mrs. Fitz and Pip walking her way.

Clodagh nodded. "Sorry, I didn't see you."

"Ah, well, Pip and I decided to take an early walk today. I think things will be a bit too busy later for a stroll." She smiled looking down at the little spaniel running around her feet. "And you, are you all ready for tonight?"

Clodagh sighed. "Nearly. Mrs. Fitz? The ghost story, about Lilly, do you think, I mean, it's so sad, the thought of her seeking her true love year after year and never finding him."

Mrs. Fitz lent on the fence next to her. "I'd like to think it isn't so bad."

Clodagh frowned. "How?"

"Well, firstly she has Veillantif." Mrs. Fitz smiled. That was true, Clodagh mused fussing over Ozzie. If she were trapped in the fairy world or wandering around as a ghost, she'd want Ozzie with her.

"And?" Clodagh asked. Mrs. Fitz glanced at her and smiled.

"If I tell you a secret, you promise not to giggle at an old lady?" Clodagh nodded; she'd never have thought about giggling at Mrs. Fitz. "I think I saw her once."

"Lilly?" Clodagh asked open-mouthed.

Mrs. Fitz looked around herself and then nodded. "In this very field. I saw her ride across the bottom of it, a misty shape like a girl on a horse, cantering. And you know what?" Clodagh shook her head. "I didn't feel sad, I thought if Lilly was a sorrowful ghost, I'd feel sad. Does that make sense?" She asked. Clodagh nodded, it did, she smiled. "And I'm not the only one who claimed to have seen her. You remember I told you about the old groom's children, the ones I was friends with." Clodagh nodded. "They saw her too, well, Dick did. He swore he saw her walking in the woods hand in hand with someone, one hand holding wispy reins as if an invisible horse was following her."

"Who?" Clodagh asked. "Who was she with?"

"I don't know," Mrs. Fitz said. "We tried to find out a little more about her."

"We did too, me and Mike, we found a record of her in the library, but not much else," Clodagh admitted.

Mrs. Fitz nodded. "We found that too, but something else as well, an old newspaper article from the year the manor was rebuilt. They reported the old ghost story with one addition, they claimed that Lilly's true love escaped that night and fled into the manor woods but he was never seen again. The reporter presumed that he had been pursued and killed, but young Elizabeth, Dick's sister, she had a different idea. She believed that the fairy folk had saved him too and that he was reunited with Lilly and that they were both allowed to return to the manor for a week."

"Being pursued and killed seems more likely," Clodagh said sadly.

"Maybe, but Elizabeth was adamant there were fairies in those woods. She'd never tell me what made her so sure, but she was." Mrs. Fitz nodded her head slowly.

"Why though? I mean if they're fairies and they saved Lilly and her true love, why would they come back at all?" Clodagh asked.

"For fun, Elizabeth said, a game, they would come back and hide in the manor and woods, recreating their lives, coming together again in the end and remembering what had happened all those years ago." Mrs. Fitz smiled.

"And what do you think?" Clodagh asked.

"I'm not sure I ever really saw her in the first place. It was so very long ago, I wasn't even your age. But I know Elizabeth was sure and maybe that's enough, besides it is a good story for this time of year." Mrs. Fitz smiled.

"I hope Elizabeth is right," Clodagh said, rubbing Ozzie's neck."

"So do I," Mrs. Fitz smiled. "Oh, goodness, look at the time. I best get Pip home."

"You could come in," Clodagh said. "Ma made Halloween breakfast."

"That sounds lovely, but I have a lot to do. I'll see you after the pumpkin ride," she said and headed off with Pip towards the manor.

Clodagh looked over at Ozzie and frowned. She had a little time before they were supposed to go into town, maybe she'd just take one last look around after breakfast. After all, she really did need to check the decorations anyway.

*

Ash pulled his coat and scarf on as Clodagh grabbed Ozzie's headcollar and pulled open the front door, stepping out of the B&B into the drab autumn morning. When she had said she was going for a quick walk around the manor before going into town he had insisted on going with her.

"So, are we ghost hunting then? Or what?" he said as she closed the door and began to walk across the drive.

She glanced at him and smiled. "I just want to have one look around before tonight. Check the decorations. Maybe bring Ozzie in so he's well rested for the ride later," she said holding up the headcollar.

Ash raised an eyebrow with her and she giggled. "Ok, yes, we're ghost hunting."

"Cool."

"Do you really need a scarf?" she asked.

"I was in the sun until a couple of days ago," he reminded her with a smile.

They headed up the driveway to the manor, checking the decorations as they went. Everything seemed to be perfect and Clodagh began to feel more and more excited about the party later on.

"It looks great," Ash said.

"I know," Clodagh grinned.

They passed the top of the paddock and into the manor grounds. They had set up a little trail of lights that directed people to the main gates, but Clodagh wandered off to one side, slipping into the old farmyard. It wasn't booked that weekend surprisingly, so the place was eerily quiet.

"Why are we here?" Ash asked. "This was built after the manor we see now right?

Clodagh nodded and headed over towards the brick wall that formed the edge of the little old farm enclosure. There was a little ledge on it that Ma had put solar lanterns on. She climbed up on it ready to look over the top of the wall.

"This is the place some people said Lilly fell or jumped," Clodagh said. "Off the ledge behind the manor."

Ash scrabbled up next to her with a smile. "Listen," Ash said trying to get her attention. "About the costume..."

Clodagh looked over the edge of the wall and froze. "Ash?" she said, her voice a little shaky.

Ash looked over the wall too, there, down below, a white streak was moving at speed towards the paddocks. Ash and Clodagh looked at each other before jumping down off the wall and running in the direction of Ozzie and Dancer's field.

*

Clodagh reached the paddock first, just in time to see the white horse break through the tree line for a second before it became just a flash of white broken by the skeletal trees, their bare branches masking it from view except for brief glimpses of white. Ash stopped beside her puffing.

"It's real," he said.

Clodagh nodded. "Too real. I think you're right, it's a loose horse."

She started to climb over the rails of the fence clutching the headcollar. He caught her arm looking confused.

"What are you doing?"

"Going after the horse," she replied.

"I don't think you'll catch it, it's fair moving." He pointed out.

She held up the headcollar. "That's why I'm taking Ozzie."

"I was afraid you were going to say that," Ash said looking worried. "What about your costume? Shouldn't we just tell your Dad, get someone to come and sort it out?"

Clodagh shook her head, she didn't care about the costume, so she'd have nothing to wear, better that than lose track of the horse. It needed help now.

"Go get some help," she said. "I promise I won't go further than the 40 acres."

She started to climb again and Ash put his foot on the fence. "I'll come with you."

Clodagh smiled. "I'm quicker with Ozzie, we'll be ok."

Ash looked at her concern etched on his face. "You sure?"

She nodded as she finished climbing the gate. "Wait, take this." Ash pulled his scarf off and handed it to her. "You can use it as another lead rope."

"Thanks." She smiled and set off jogging across the field whistling to Ozzie as she did. Ozzie twirled at the sound of her voice and cantered flat out towards her, sensing she needed him fast. He covered the field in what seemed like seconds, his mane and tail flowing out behind him as he ran.

Behind her, Clodagh instinctively knew Ash was running too, heading to the manor. Clodagh scrambled onto the fence next to Ozzie and quickly fastened his headcollar on.

"Someone needs our help," she said as she slid onto his back.

They turned as one towards the bottom of the paddock and cantered towards the old gate in the far corner of the field. Dancer was running up and down the fence line calling to them, but Ozzie didn't falter, following Clodagh's signals without hesitation.

They pulled up to the gate and with a look over her shoulder to check on Ash, Clodagh unlatched the gate and threw it wide open. She and Ozzie rode out into the woods, surrounded by solar light strings set up for the pumpkin trail.

"Which way," she mused.

The horse had been heading towards the end of the woods, but she doubted it would have run onto the road or over to Briary if it had been hanging around this long. No, Clodagh thought, they'd have gone down to the brook, over that side of the woods. That's why she'd seen the hoof marks there. She'd been right, they weren't Ozzie's. She remembered back to seeing the grey horse in the woods and forty acres, it had to be the same one and not Gracie's as she'd convinced herself. After a second, she and Ozzie turned towards the manor and cantered quickly along the trail towards the fork and the brook.

Chapter 9

Clodagh and Ozzie charged through the brook, water spraying up as Ozzie's hooves pounded through the stream. The spray hit Clodagh's legs in little cold splatters, but she ignored it focusing only on the track ahead. They barely paused as they started up the incline towards the forty acres. Breaking out of the woods into the open, Clodagh eased Ozzie up and the pair of them stared out over the expanse of field in front of them. The faded yellowing grass waved a little in the slightly cool breeze, standing out starkly against the blue-grey October sky. There was no sign of the grey horse anywhere.

"Where did it go?" Clodagh said aloud.

Ozzie tossed his head to one side, giving a little tug on the lead rope she held in one hand. "Ok," she said. "We'll try that way."

They turned in the direction Ozzie had suggested, following the edge of the woods. This part of the forty acres didn't have a very clear path along it. Since Ozzie had arrived, Dad had cut a neat little path from the edge of the woodland trail to the gate that opened onto the road, opposite which were the fields Briary rented from the manor. It made a nice little circular hack for them. He'd added another path from the same gate to a hole in the hedge Gracie had widened a little while back, so some days, when she had company, they could hack to the old McDonald place too. The far side of the field though, that was left to grow all summer and cut for hay. As a result, it was hardly ever somewhere Clodagh and Ozzie went. Now though, at his suggestion, they rode up beside the thick spindly trees.

Clodagh started to look through the woods, trying to glimpse anything white. At first, she thought they had lost the horse completely, but then, she saw it. A grey shape stood in a little clearing, breathing heavily. The woods in that part of the manor were pretty much left wild and it took Clodagh a while to find a way into the little clearing. The branches hung low and as she and Ozzie began to pick their way through, Clodagh thought back to the la trec course they had done in the summer.

"It's just like the la trec," she said quietly as much to herself as to Ozzie. Only without a saddle or bridle, she added to herself.

As they drew closer the strange horse raised its head, his ears flicking. Clodagh instinctively went quiet. Her Aunt Lisa had always told her to be quiet when out on a ride if she wanted to see the wildlife. Most creatures, Aunt Lisa said, saw a horse, not a horse and rider, unless the rider was making a ruckus. It had been proven true to Clodagh more than once.

The grey horse whickered and Ozzie whickered back, his neat ears swivelling like mini radars. Ozzie picked his way around a few more trees and into the clearing and for the first time Clodagh saw the strange horse clearly. She gasped and then clamped a hand over her mouth remembering she was trying to be quiet. The horse in front of her looked very much like a lighter grey Ozzie! Its small neat head and ears had a similar look, even their builds were alike, only Ozzie had darker dapples, the pony in front of her was almost white, though his lower legs and tail held hints of a darker, more silvery shade of grey.

"He's a Connie," Clodagh breathed quietly, one hand on Ozzie's neck.

Suddenly it all made sense. Clodagh thought back to the phone call Mrs. Fitz had received from Angela. The stud owner had only said her stallion had gotten out, not specifically that it was Zeus, she had just assumed it was. When Clodagh had visited before, Angela had mentioned she had a Connemara stallion as well, but he was out on loan at the time and not due back for a few more weeks. That had been several months ago. Clodagh looked at the pony with fresh eyes and nodded to herself. She was pretty sure she was looking at Angela's Connemara stallion.

"Ok," she said to herself, taking a deep breath.

She urged Ozzie into the clearing and the two ponies greeted each other with little snorts and sniffs. It was clear they had met before and Clodagh hoped that was going to help her now. She hadn't exactly gone any further than she had told Ash she would, but she wasn't certain they'd locate her here quickly and they'd probably start shouting her name and scare the pony in the process. Clodagh started to think quickly. She could ride Ozzie back and get help, but would the stallion stay in the clearing? Should she try and catch him maybe? Then she could tie him up using Ash's scarf.

She realised suddenly though, that wouldn't work. The horse could panic and break free, then he'd be running around with something trailing along he could stand on. She wondered if she could fashion the scarf into a headcollar and use that on Ozzie, while leading the stallion on Ozzie's headcollar and lead rope. Clodagh looked back the way they had come through the narrow passage and bit her lip. It was definitely only one horse wide, with two long ropes she could do it, but not with one rope and a headcollar, she couldn't stretch that far. There was only one way to get them all out of here, together, at once and she knew it.

"Ok, Ozzie, going to need your help buddy," she said.

Slowly she slid off Ozzie and stood beside him. The stallion looked at her and snorted a little, but she stayed calm and stood still, hoping that seeing Ozzie trusted her, the stallion might too.

Slowly she unclipped Ozzie's lead rope and fastened it around his neck, then slipped off his head collar. Ozzie stood patiently as

Clodagh took hold of the rope around his neck and took a step towards the stallion. The strange grey horse's head lifted an inch and Clodagh dropped her gaze so she wasn't looking him dead in the eye. Ozzie slowly followed her toward him.

"Easy boy," she said holding her hand out just a little to the strange horse.

Twigs and sticks snapped as they moved and with every leaf rustle, Clodagh worried the stallion would spook and bolt, but he stayed still watching her a little warily. Soon enough they were close enough to touch. Clodagh stopped still and stretched her hand out towards him, palm up. Slowly, cautiously, the stallion reached out his nose to her hand. His soft grey muzzle snuffled across her palm. Clodagh inched forward again, gradually touching his neck. She hoped he liked scratches as much as Ozzie did.

Clodagh began to scratch the horse's neck, just gently and he leaned into her, his nose twisting a little, his lip wiggling back and forth. She let out a little laugh and looked at Ozzie who was standing by her shoulder.

"He likes it too," she said to him. "You do, don't you, is that a spot? Yes? See, you're ok, you're ok with us, isn't he Ozzie."

She stood in the clearing for what seemed like an hour just scratching and petting the stallion, letting him know he was safe and she could be trusted. Then, when she was sure he was used to her, she carefully slid Ozzie's headcollar over his head. It fitted perfectly and she looked again from one to the other. They looked so similar, it was so strange.

"Ok, we're going to get out of here now alright?" she said looking from one to the other. "We'll go steady together, get you some food, bet you're hungry." The stallion snorted. "I'm trusting you guys."

Clodagh very slowly took the scarf Ash had given her from around her shoulders and slid it around Ozzie's neck, fastening it with a knot at his withers.

"Thanks, Ash," she said as she clipped Ozzie's rope onto the head collar she had slipped onto the stallion.

"Ok boys, we're going to ride out of here nice and easy." She led Ozzie to a fallen log, keeping hold of the rope in her hand and over Ozzie's back, she climbed onto the log. Swallowing she prepared to hop up on Ozzie hoping it wouldn't spook the stallion.

"I hope you know how to ride and lead," she said to the Ozzie look alike. "Ok, Ozzie."

She smiled as Ozzie stamped a foot and she hopped up onto his back. Luckily the stallion seemed unphased by her move and she settled herself onto Ozzie's back. Not for the first time, she was glad that despite being teased about it, she had started riding Ozzie with no tack at all. It had come in useful more times now than she cared to remember. She gripped the scarf as an extra precaution, she may trust Ozzie and might have ridden him like this before, but never while leading a strange stallion. Besides, with it she could lean back under some of the low branches while keeping hold of the stallion's rope.

"Let's go steady," she said urging Ozzie forwards towards the little trail they'd come in on.

Ozzie started to move up the narrow track, following the path, while Clodagh tried to remember to duck the branches while holding onto the lead rope. Surprisingly, now he was caught, the stallion seemed more than happy to follow Ozzie through the tangle of branches. A few times Clodagh was sure she'd scratched her face and her hair caught in a branch, but eventually, they managed to find their way out into the big field again.

Out of the woods, the stallion tried to jog a little and Clodagh gently pulled the lead rope so he came up alongside Ozzie.

"Ok, steady, just walk," she said. He flicked his ears at her but began to walk next to Ozzie.

Steering with her seat and legs, Clodagh guided Ozzie back towards the main trail through the woods, hoping Ash would appear with every step. They reached the big gap that marked the entrance to the woods again and set off down towards the brook. The stallion snorted a lot, eyeing up the strings of solar lights and pumpkins they had put out for the trail ride later and Clodagh began to wonder if that was what had set his flight off earlier that morning. Something had clearly spooked him when she had spotted him from the farm wall, but then she realised where he had been didn't have any lights, it wasn't part of the trail. She pushed the thought to one side, it didn't really matter what had frightened him so long as he'd been caught. Now they just needed to focus on safely getting them home.

They had almost reached the brook when she heard Ash calling her name. "By the streams" she called back and then, having thought about it, added "and don't run!"

Ash appeared at the fork just as they reached the stream itself. "Wait there," he called walking down towards them. Clodagh had Ozzie stop and waited until Ash reached them. Behind him, she could see Melissa and Sam dashing to catch up.

"I'll take him," Ash said, eyeing up the Connemara. "Hey big lad, you've been having quite the adventure huh?"

The stallion regarded him carefully but again, seeing Ozzie happily attacking Ash's pockets for a carrot, seemed to relax. Clodagh passed Ash the horse's rope.

"You go first," Ash said. "I'll lead him behind you."

Clodagh smiled. "Thanks."

She and Ozzie crossed the stream, with Ash and the stallion right behind. Sam and Melissa had come to a stop at the fork and were staring at them in shock and surprise.

"You know," Ash said from behind. "You and Ozzie could do stunt work riding like that."

Clodagh smiled, she turned to look over her shoulder. "You might need to wash your scarf."

He chuckled. "I think Ozzie should keep it, it suits him."

Ozzie snorted loudly and Clodagh giggled.

"What the heck is going on?" Sam asked as they reached the fork.

"Where's Dad?" Clodagh asked.

"Out getting the last things for tonight," Sam said. "Who's the Ozzie look alike?"

"Guys, I'd like you to meet Angela's missing stallion. At least I think that's who it is. Sam, if you have your phone could you please call Mrs. Fitz and tell her what's going on, oh and ask if it was Zeus who got out?"

"Zeus?" Sam asked.

"Zeus. If she says no, can you tell her we have Angela's Connie stallion?" Clodagh said.

Sam looked confused but pulled his phone out and started dialling as the whole party started to walk back towards the Manor.

"Well, this is not what I expected to do today." Melissa smiled.

Clodagh froze on Ozzie. Melissa was here. She looked over at the girl in horror. "You, you were supposed to go with Ma, to get things from town to finish your costume!"

"Eh, it's ok," Melissa shrugged. "I have some purple ribbon, I just thought blue would go better, it's no big deal, not when Ash came running in spouting off about loose horses and phantom stallions. The bigger problem is you don't have a costume for tonight."

Clodagh sighed and looked back over her shoulder to where Ash was happily chatting away to the stallion. The horse seemed totally relaxed with Ash, following him along easily, the rope swinging as they went, his neck lower.

"It doesn't matter," Clodagh smiled. "I found the phantom horse and he's safe. That's more important. I'll just put on that old witch's hat and some black clothes, it won't be the best costume in the world, but it'll be just fine."

She smiled as Ozzie headed up towards the manor gardens. Through the rhododendrons, she could see Mrs. Fitz flinging open the orangery door and heading across to them quickly. Sam, up in front, turned around and gave her a thumbs up. It seemed like she had been right, this was Angela's wayward stallion.

Clodagh patted Ozzie as the troop turned to step into the gardens and down below them, just where they had seen the stallion start to run, just for one second, Clodagh could have sworn she saw a wispy grey shape move through the trees. She shook her head and giggled, this time her mind really was playing tricks on her.

Chapter 10

Clodagh pulled her witches hat out of the top of her closet and put it on her bed next to her black school skirt and a purple sweater with a sigh. After they had arrived back at the manor, she had learnt that the stallion, the Ozzie look-alike was actually called Merlin and he was indeed Angela's missing Connemara stallion. He had been put in one of the manor stables along with Ozzie and Dancer until Angela could come and pick him up later. Both Ozzie and Dancer had started eating as soon as they were in, but Merlin had laid down in the shavings, rolled, and then promptly fallen asleep.

It had taken a little explaining on Clodagh's part as to how she had discovered him. She felt rather silly confessing she'd suspected he was a phantom horse, but since she had never really got a good look at him until that day, everyone seemed to understand. Mrs. Fitz did make her promise to tell her if she saw something in the future though, even if Clodagh did think it was a ghost. Clodagh had happily agreed.

Sam had promised to stay and keep an eye on Merlin while Clodagh, Melissa, and Ash ran home to change and get ready for the pumpkin ride and Mrs. Fitz sorted out turning on the lanterns and various fake candles in the manor ahead of the party. Clodagh had sent a text to both Rachel and Beth explaining very briefly what had happened and that she still didn't have a costume. Beth had rung her a little while later and offered to lend her a pair of stripy purple tights she had from a costume the year before. Together with the hat, skirt, and jumper, Clodagh thought she'd make a passible witch, especially if she could persuade Ma to lend her the old-fashioned broom from the downstairs cleaning closet.

"Clodagh," Ma called from downstairs. "You'd best go fetch Ozzie love, or you'll be late."

Grabbing a clean jumper, Clodagh darted out of her room and raced towards the stairs. Ash came out of his room and waved at her as she jogged past.

"I'll meet you and Melissa at Briary," she smiled without stopping. "Sandra knows you're coming, just give her your names. Beth should be there by the time you walk down, but if not and you need help Charlotte will be for sure."

Ash opened his mouth as if he was going to say something, but Clodagh was already flying down the stairs to grab her coat and Ozzie's tack.

Merlin was awake by the time Clodagh got back to the manor, he stood placidly in the stable munching hay and watching Sam over the stable door.

"He really does look like Ozzie," Sam said to her as she jogged over. "You think that's because they're both the same breed?"

"Must be," Clodagh said. She'd seen a lot of Connemaras in pictures, some grey, some dun, a lot of them had similar features, build, and so on, but none of the ones she had seen had looked quite so alike as Merlin and Ozzie did. Still, there were a lot more Connemaras in the world than she had seen on the internet. Some, she guessed, were bound to look similar to one and another.

"You getting ready to head down to the trail?" Sam asked. Clodagh nodded. "Right, Rachel's here, she's in with Dancer now. I'll nip home and grab my costume and then head to the trail, I'm on bridge duty. I think Merlin here will be ok, he seems pretty relaxed."

"Ok, we'll see you in a bit," Clodagh smiled and while Sam set off towards the B&B, she darted around the corner to the box Ozzie occupied.

Rachel's head popped over the door, a look of relief washing over her face. "You're late, I thought I might have to ride down on my own."

Clodagh smiled. "I'll be ready in five minutes."

"While you're getting ready," Rachel said as Clodagh slipped into Ozzie's stable, "you can tell me about Merlin." Clodagh smiled, that was going to be an interesting story to tell.

Ten minutes later Clodagh stepped up the mounting block and hopped onto Ozzie, as Rachel tightened Dancer's girth up.

"You really led an unknown stallion while riding bareback with no bridle?" Rachel asked for the second time.

"He wasn't exactly unknown," Clodagh mused. "I was pretty sure at that point he was Angela's."

"But you didn't *know him*," Rachel said. Clodagh shrugged. "Plus, bareback with no bridle."

"On Ozzie," Clodagh pointed out. Rachel rolled her eyes a little. "It's not a big deal."

"Oh, it is," Rachel said. "Maybe you don't see it, but it is."

They rode out of the yard together waving at Merlin who popped his head over the door, a bit of hay hanging from his mouth, and headed down the drive chatting. It was a short ride down to Briary, but even so, Clodagh could tell it was darker when they arrived at the riding school than it had been when they set off from the manor. The timing would be perfect. It should just be dark enough when the ride reached the woods for the solar lights to have come on.

Beth and Maverick were waiting for them by the wicket gate that led into the riding school when they reached it. Behind her, amid a mass of ponies, kids of varying ages, and some parents, Clodagh caught sight of Ash and Melissa and waved. They both smiled and waved back. Clodagh noticed Angela had put Melissa on a little chestnut mare she'd seen before, while Ash had Benji, the little bay Welshie Clodagh had once recommended Sandra buy at the same sale she had bought Ozzie.

Sandra spotted them and came over leading a large bay thoroughbred with a white star. She smiled at them brightly.

"I hear you and Ozzie have been on another adventure," she said and Clodagh smiled, instinctively rubbing Ozzie's neck. "I'd like to hear that story later."

"We promise she'll tell it," Beth smiled.

"How do you want to organise the ride?" Clodagh asked, changing the subject.

Sandra took a deep breath. "Well, I'd say you and Ozzie earned the right to lead. If half of the things I heard about your adventure today and in the summer are true I think you're more than capable. Besides, you laid out the route. How about you, Rachel and Beth take the lead, I'll get Jessica my head girl to follow you and lead the riding school troop and I'll bring up the rear with Eden here. We'll pop the lead rein ponies in the middle." She patted the bay mare.

"Sounds good to us," Beth said. "Eh Mav."

Maverick poured the ground and snorted as if the whole thing needed to move a lot faster for his liking. Clodagh giggled and turned Ozzie around ready to go.

"All right, everyone mount up if you aren't already," Sandra called putting her foot in her stirrup and leaping up on the bay mare. "Clodagh is in the lead with Rachel and Beth, Jessica will be behind, I'm caboose. Lead rein ponies, in the middle please, don't lose your parents, we don't want to have to send out a search party." A lot of the lead rein kids started to laugh. "I have it on good authority that there will be a special surprise for our junior riders." Clodagh frowned wondering what that was about. She hadn't set up any surprise. "Any problems call up. Sally," A girl on a little dun pony looked up. "Try not to let Hamish eat the pumpkins. We do not want a repeat of this morning." The girl giggled and if ever a pony could look guilty, Hamish did. Clodagh smiled, making a mental note to ask exactly what Hamish had done later.

"Here we go," Clodagh said and turned Ozzie towards home.

The little ride from Briary to the manor was not very Halloween-themed. They hadn't strung lights or anything, mostly because it was the way to Sandra's turn-out fields and they hadn't wanted to put anything in her way, but once they got to the manor gates it was a different story. Two carved pumpkins, lit with flickering fake candles had been sat by each pillar, and a further two had been stuck on the spikes of the black wrought iron gates. They glowed, very faintly in the dusky light. There were murmurs and giggles from behind and Clodagh smiled. Ma waved at her from the front window and Clodagh waved back.

The ride past the B&B and turned along the little track that led to the gate to Ozzie's paddock, before turning and following the fence along the bottom edge of the field. Ozzie strode out happily, leading the ride towards the woods. Stepping into the tree line, Clodagh caught sight of the trail ride fully lit up and smiled broadly, everything had worked out perfectly. The strings of little orange fairy lights illuminated the way, washing the track in a strange, but pleasant light. Every now and then there was a pumpkin dotted about, some carved, others not. They sat at the base of the trees in amongst the tangled roots, or up in the branches. One had even been set up like a scarecrow with a smiling pumpkin face and an old straw hat. Clodagh suspected the hat might have been an old one of Ma's. It had a large pink flower stuck to the front of it that didn't match the denim dungarees the scarecrow wore at all.

Besides the pumpkins, as they rode through the trees, there were other things to see too. One tree had been given a face. Dad had made it from old plywood and some leftover paint and tacked it to the tree with some nails. All of the riders giggled and pointed as they passed it and Clodagh felt proud. Sure in the light of day it looked a little cobbled together, but right then, in the darkening evening, surrounded by the orange lights, it looked very good indeed.

The trail reached the fork and Clodagh turned down towards the stream. Before she could get there, however, Sam appeared standing in the way and halting the ride. He was dressed as a pirate, with a pair of brown battered trousers, an oversized white shirt, and a large tricorne hat. A plastic cutlass hung from his belt.

"Avast young riders," he said.

Beth giggled. "I thought you were going to the party as one of those warcraft people."

Sam winked at her. "Thought you'd like this more." He smiled, and so did Beth while Clodagh fought to keep a straight face.

"Now maties, any young riders here who have parents with them?" he called.

There were shouts of yes from some of the kids and some of the parents. Sam smiled, clearly enjoying his part.

"Well now, we don't want those parents getting soaked in the stream before the party now do we?"

Some of the kids shouted 'YES', but most said no, with their parents agreeing. Sam pulled up his trousers to reveal long wellingtons. He tucked the brown corduroys into them.

"Well now, how about I lead you across my stream while the parents walk the plank." He gestured to the bridge and there were cheers all around. "And any of my young maties who complete the ride will have to tell my pirate mate at the end of the ride, see if he can't give you a few doubloons to start your trick or treating off!" Sam headed down to the bridge to wait for the first lead rein pony, while Clodagh and the others splashed through the water.

"Did you know about this?" Beth asked her when they were across.

"Nope," Clodagh replied.

"Who's his pirate mate?" Rachel asked. Clodagh shrugged.

It took a little while to ferry the lead rein ponies over the stream, but everyone agreed it was a great way of doing it and Sam was brilliant with the little kids, even having his picture taken with a couple of them. Clodagh and Ozzie then lead the ride up and out of the woods into the forty-acre field. Here there were no strings of lights, but Dad was standing by the gate dressed as a highwayman and holding up a large lantern for them to ride towards. He held the gate open for everyone to pass through, closing it and the gate on the opposite side of the road that led back to Briary when they had passed through it.

This last stretch of the track did have a few pumpkins along it, but they were not what caught Clodagh's attention. What did was a brightly lit area right at the end of the ride. Sat in a pool of light was a large treasure chest Clodagh knew well. It had been her and Sam's toy box when they were little children. Now it sat illuminated by one of Dad's work lamps. On it, dressed in full pirate gear was Mike, holding up a jolly roger flag. Clodagh laughed as they drew near and he waved.

"Can I assume you are a pirate matey?" she asked.

Mike smiled. "Aye, you can." He gave his best pirate impression. "It was your Dad's idea, cool huh?"

"I love it," Clodagh smiled.

The riders gathered around, and while the older ones took their horses back to the stables and went to change for the party, the younger ones clustered around Mike. He handed out chocolate coins from the chest to each one and then they were led away by happy, smiling parents.

"This was amazing," Sandra said coming over. "We should do it every year."

Clodagh nodded. It seemed like a new tradition at the manor might just have been born. Dad walked up with Sam and hugged Clodagh.

"Well done. Now, you three best get those horses back up to the manor," he said looking at Clodagh, Rachel, and Beth. "Then get back to the B&B to get changed ready to help out with the kid's party. Oh, and leave your costumes for the main event ready, you'll need to get changed into them quickly. I think we have one more surprise in store for you all tonight."

"What?" Clodagh asked.

Dad sighed. "Oh, I was going to keep it a secret, but I need to tell Sandra anyway, so…" Everyone had gathered around him to listen. "Ok, anyone here with a ticket to the main party, not the children's one I'm afraid, I know you were planning on parking at Sandra's and walking up to the manor, but there has been a bit of a change in plan. If you can walk to the B&B and wait there you'll be collected and taken up in groups."

"How?" Beth asked.

"By coach," Dad smiled. "As a thank you to Clodagh for finding Merlin, Angela Hart from the Woodlea Stud will be driving everyone that went on the ride up to the manor in the old gig with Zeus and Troy. I may even have time to do a few Halloween modifications to it," he mused, rubbing his chin. Audible gasps of excitement went around the crowd. "But the first trip from the B&B is reserved for you," he smiled at Clodagh and her friends. "So, you best get moving," Dad said.

Clodagh stared at Dad for a second, not quite sure she'd heard him correctly. They were really going to get to ride in the big old gig up the party, it sounded too good to be true.

Chapter 11

Clodagh pulled on her best pair of jeans and glanced at the witch costume lying on her bed with a sigh. Somehow the idea of turning up to the manor in a cobbled-together witches outfit in the old gig seemed wrong. Clodagh picked up the hat sadly turning it in her hands and then thought back to Merlin standing happily eating hay in the stable and she smiled.

"Are you ok?" Rachel asked. Clodagh looked over at her as she put the hat back down on the bed and nodded. At least she and Rachel would sort of match. Rachel had opted to go as a black cat, with little ears on her headband and a long fluffy tail. Clodagh and Beth had used face paints to give her a little pink nose and black whiskers. It was cute and Halloween like all-in-one go.

Clodagh smiled. "Yeah. I was just thinking it would have been nice to turn up in a proper costume since we're riding in this fancy gig to this amazingly decorated party."

"You mean rather than wearing your school skirt," Beth said, nodding her understanding.

Clodagh sighed. "But it's worth it. Merlin's safe."

Rachel and Beth grabbed her in a hug and Clodagh smiled. "We could use the face paints to paint you green?" Rachel suggested, but Clodagh shook her head. She didn't mind being a witch, but she didn't want to be a green one.

"You know you could just put your costume on now like the rest of us," Beth said as she twirled around a little in her pirate costume and Clodagh smiled; she'd look brilliant side by side with Sam.

"Thanks, but I think I'll put it on later. I promised Dad I'd man the apple bobbing; I am going to get wet," she sighed.

"Hey, I forgot to ask," Rachel said turning to Beth with a grin. "Are you the captain or is Sam?"

Beth giggled and adjusted the red sash she had tied around her waist. "Both of us, rival ships."

"Oh, forbidden love." Rachel laughed.

Clodagh giggled. There was a knock on the door and Melissa poked her head through.

"You guys ready?" she asked, her eyes dancing with excitement.

"Almost." Clodagh pulled open her wardrobe, scanned the contents, grabbed a cardigan, and pulled it on. "Done."

"Cool, let's go."

They bustled out into the hall. "Wow," Clodagh said, catching sight of Melissa's outfit for the first time. "Your costume is awesome."

Melissa spun around, the little pale green and yellow skirt of her dress, with its ragged hem, flaring out as she did. Her hair was perfectly curled, with bits coloured green for the night. Even her makeup was flawless, her cheeks and eyes covered in slightly sparkling shades of the colours in her dress and wings. "It's cool huh," she smiled. "I didn't put my fairy wings on yet though, I could do with a hand tying them on actually."

She held up a pair of golden sparkly wings, with little bits of ribbon hanging from them. Clodagh took them from her and began to fasten them to the back of Melissa's costume.

"There," she said.

"Thanks, Ash said he'd help me with them, but he said he had to go do something," she shrugged.

"Where is Ash?" Rachel asked.

"He said he'd meet us up at the hall when he'd sorted something out," Melissa said.

"You guys come on," Sam shouted from downstairs. "The party starts in ten minutes."

They all hurried down the stairs to where Sam stood, still in his pirate costume, waiting for them. He ushered them out of the door, closing it behind him.

*

A little girl with long blond pigtails dressed as a cute little rag doll, popped up in front of Clodagh, spilling water all around as she did. The girl beamed as she took the bright red apple from her mouth.

"Winner!" Clodagh smiled, handing her a chocolate coin. "You can keep the apple too."

The little girl took the coin and squealed, bouncing up and down and rushing to her mother shoving both the coin and apple at her. The woman hugged her and smiled over at Clodagh.

"Next," Clodagh waved a little boy over to take his turn.

The party was in full swing and seemed to be going really well. All of the children seemed to be having a fantastic time and Clodagh was too, watching them in their costumes enjoying the games and music.

Mike, who was manning a popcorn machine across the room, caught her eye and waved. He'd come dressed as a skeleton, but added a red bow tie so he 'looked formal'. Alice was standing with him dressed as a white rabbit with a pink tail and tummy. They looked decidedly odd together, but they looked very happy too. She smiled and waved back at them both. The little boy dunked his head into the bucket of apples, slightly spraying Clodagh with a shower of water, she gasped and giggled a little.

Beth ambled over to her with a smile. "Your Ma asked if I'd take over for you for a bit so you could grab a drink and maybe a snack. I know there's food later, but the cake is awesome!"

"Thanks," Clodagh smiled. "I might just pop out and check on Ozzie and Merlin too,"

Leaving Beth to deal with the little boy, she headed over to the table of food. Her eyes danced over all of the nice things there. Ma had outdone herself with the kid's food. There were hot dogs made to look like fingers, spaghetti labelled worms, and olives filled with cheese she had put a sign saying eyeballs on. There was even a pile of mini marshmallow ghosts with chocolate eyes, and in the middle of all of it, a stand full of cupcakes made to look like little pumpkins.

Clodagh picked one up and helped herself to a glass of lemonade turned green with food dye, before she headed towards the door.

The library was hot and loud and Clodagh sighed at the cool peacefulness of the hallway. As much fun as it was to help out with the kids, it was so loud she could barely think. Clodagh nibbled at the cake as she headed out into the manor courtyard. As soon as she appeared, Ozzie's head popped over the door and he whickered at her.

She skipped over to him, stuffing the last of the cake in her mouth as she went. He nuzzled at her hand and licked at the little bit of icing left on her fingers. She scratched his neck.

"Guess you're enjoying Halloween," she said.

"I'd say so,"

Clodagh spun around in surprise to see Ash standing behind her, lurking in the shadows. "Where have you been? The party's nearly over."

Ash smiled at her, "I had a couple of things to sort out. How's the party going?"

Clodagh frowned, wanting to ask 'what things' but decided not to. "The part's great, the kids got a real kick out of seeing Melissa. Are you going to surprise them too?"

He nodded and stepped out of the shadow of the stable so she could see his costume better. Clodagh beamed. She recognised it immediately as one he'd worn in the film. They had used the manor as a location for. It was perfect for the party too, the baggy cream shirt, waistcoat, and trousers made him look like he'd gone for a sort of medieval costume.

"I'll take that as a yes," she said waving at the costume, he smiled. "Come on."

She was about to head back inside when the sound of an engine on the drive stopped her. Grabbing Ash's arm, she raced to the gate just in time to see Angela's wagon roll to a stop. She waved as she hopped out of the cab.

"Clodagh!"

Clodagh ran over. "Hi."

Angela hugged her. "I hear I owe you a ride."

Clodagh smiled. "Merlin's inside, we left Ozzie and Dancer in to keep him company."

"Thanks," Angela said. "I brought Zeus and Troy. Is there somewhere I can pop them while we sort out the gig?"

"Yep," Dad said coming up behind them. "The farm boxes are empty; the guest there doesn't mind."

Clodagh frowned, she hadn't realised anyone was staying on the farm over Halloween, but she pushed the thought out of her head.

"You two better get back to the kid's party, there isn't very long left now," Dad said.

Clodagh nodded and headed back inside with Ash, glancing back over her shoulder as they went.

There was a roar and squeals of delight when they re-entered the party and the kids saw that Ash was there as well as Melissa. The pair even had pictures taken with anyone who wanted one. The music was turned up just a little and the lights dimmed so that the place was illuminated more by pumpkin light apart from one spot near the cake table. The parish clerk came out with Halloween pass the parcel and pin the hat on the witch before the festivities began to draw to a close.

Ma cleared her throat. "Well, everyone, we hope you have had a great time tonight." There were cheers from the children. "Now, before everyone heads home, we have two things left. First, in a moment, our celebrity guest judge Melissa Hutchins is going to announce the winners of the costume competition," Melissa waved her hand and the kids clapped. "And then, before you go, please see one of my pirate helpers for a special treat." Sam and Beth waved and Clodagh noticed they had been making up little bags of sweets for the kids. "All right, I'll hand you over to Melissa."

Melissa stepped forwards and stood next to Ma with a smile. She looked around the kids all stood in their Halloween costumes. "Oh, this was so tough, you all look awesome! But, I only get to give out three prizes. So, in third place is," she looked around the room eventually pointing to the little girl dressed as a rag doll. "Raggedy Anne."

The little girl squealed in delight and ran over. She hugged Melissa, who smiled at her and handed over a huge gold chocolate coin as big as the girl's hand. The little girl's eyes widened and she walked back to her mother staring at the glittering coin.

"In second place," Melissa scanned the crowd. "Oh, got to be my friend over there riding a t-rex."

A little boy dressed like a park ranger riding a puppet T-rex looked so surprised Clodagh had to stifle a giggle. He strode forward pretending he was struggling to control the dinosaur and Melissa smiled, playing along and telling the dinosaur he should behave himself. She handed the boy another coin and he walked back to his cheering friends.

"And finally, first place has to be the pumpkin." A little boy of about eight dressed as a pumpkin began to bounce up and down in excitement. He ran up to Melissa eagerly and she handed him the last coin."

"Ok everyone, thank you for having us at your party," Melissa smiled.

Everyone began to cheer and wave. Ma stepped up to Clodagh. "Best get yourself back to the B&B and get changed. The others need to head down too if they want to ride in the gig. I'll sort this lot out with the parish helpers."

Clodagh nodded and started rounding everyone up to head back down to the B&B. As they slipped out into the hall, Clodagh noticed Mrs. Fitz stood by the library wall, a smile on her face as she watched all of the children finishing their Halloween fun and taking their bags of candy. It made Clodagh smile too.

*

Since everyone was already in their costumes except Clodagh, Sam suggested they sit outside B&B on the wooden bench. It was surprisingly mild for the time of year and had been so hot in the manor that everyone readily agreed. As Clodagh pushed open the door though she noticed Ash and Melissa talking conspiratorially to one side and frowned when Melissa looked her way with a smile.

With a shrug, she headed inside and started up the stairs towards her bedroom. It wouldn't be so bad being a witch, sure she would look a little roughly done compared to her friends, but it didn't matter, they'd have fun no matter what. The sound of the front door closing again made her pause on the stairs, she glanced back to see Ash coming in.

"Hold up," he called. Clodagh stopped and he jogged up the stairs to her. "You can't go to the party in a cobbled-together costume and an old cardboard witches hat."

Clodagh smiled. "It's ok, I don't mind, besides I don't have a lot of choices, it's either that or I go in my jeans. Oh, unless Melissa did her makeup really well, do you think she'd do mine? I have some face paint, maybe she could make me a ghost or a zombie or something?"

Ash shook his head with a smile. "Come on."

She followed him upstairs and waited on the landing while he disappeared into his room. A few seconds later he reappeared with a garment bag in his hands. He handed it to her.

"What's this?" she asked.

"Open it."

Clodagh hung the bag over the railings of the stairs and pulled down the zipper. Inside was a beautiful red velvet medieval-style dress with gold trim. She gasped.

"It might not be a perfect fit," Ash said. "But it should be pretty close."

Clodagh stood silently staring at the dress before turning to Ash confused. "I, but, how?"

He smiled. "I called Nick, remember, I told you he was doing Shakespeare. Well, the costume lady working on the play is the same one who worked on Mists. I called in a favour. It's just on loan for tonight."

"Are you serious!" Clodagh said breaking out into a huge smile, he nodded. "Thank you!"

She flung herself onto Ash and he hugged her back. "Go, you best get changed."

"I'll help," Melissa said jogging up the stairs, her golden wings waving.

"Thank you!" Clodagh squealed, hugging her too.

"Oh no, this is all him. I just found out," She smiled. "But I am doing your hair and makeup. Do you have makeup?"

"Erm, I have face paint."

"Come with me," Melissa said steering Clodagh towards her room. "This could take a little while." She smiled at Ash, he rolled his eyes and wandered back downstairs.

*

Clodagh could hear the rumbling of the gig's wheels on the driveway as she reached out for the door handle. She took a deep breath, her fingers resting on the cold brass. Behind her, Melissa smiled and nodded. Clodagh turned the handle and opened the door.

Everyone turned to look at her as she stepped out into the night. Beth and Rachel both gasped and then hugged each other. Mike and

Alice looked both surprised and pleased, even Ash looked a little taken aback. Sam wandered over and hugged her.

"About time you got to be a princess for the night little sis, but makeup is just for tonight, ok?" He said, she smiled at him and gently slapped his arm.

The gig had turned and pulled up outside the B&B and they all walked over toward it. Dad had strewn a few fake cobwebs on the outside and put fake glowing pumpkins at both the front and back. Zeus and Troy stood proudly ready to take their passengers on the short trip.

As they got closer though, Clodagh realised it wasn't Angela who sat in the driver's seat. Mrs. Fitz looked down and smiled at them, especially Clodagh.

"Mrs. Fitz?" Clodagh asked.

"Special Halloween treat for me from Angela. She's lending me, Zeus and Troy, for the night, I'm lending her the gig for a family wedding in the spring." She lent down a little. "Haven't felt this young in years." She smiled. "Now, Lady Clodagh, shall we go?"

The others began to step into the gig, but Clodagh paused. She bit her lip looking up at Mrs. Fitz.

"May I, may I ride with you?" she asked.

Mrs. Fitz beamed. "Of course, you can. I would be delighted. Young man?" she called to Ash. He looked at her with a grin. "Would you be so kind as to help Clodagh up, it's not easy in a gown."

Ash took Clodagh's hand and helped her up onto the seat next to Mrs. Fitz. Clodagh looked over at her. In the ark, with only the moon as a light, she somehow seemed younger. With a flick of the reins and a click of her tongue, Mrs. Fitz set Troy and Zeus off up the driveway towards the manor.

Chapter 12

Mrs. Fitz pulled the gig to a stop just outside of the manor's huge green wooden gates. Clodagh sat looking around herself with a huge smile on her face. The moonlight glinted off the gig's side and illuminated the manor gates, bathing them in silver. Troy snorted and Zeus pawed the ground a little with a hoof as everyone began to climb out, eager to get going again.

"Thanks, Mrs. Fitz," Clodagh said as she climbed down with the help of Ash. Mrs. Fitz was right, climbing on and off the gig in a dress was not the easiest thing to do.

"You are more than welcome. I think this may be the best Halloween I've ever had," Mrs. Fitz said with a smile. She lent down to Clodagh. "If I was just a few years younger, I might even be tempted to take up driving again." She let out a little giggle as she picked up the reins once more and set the boys off again to pick up the next guests that would be waiting at the B&B.

Clodagh smiled as she watched Mrs. Fitz head off into the night. She turned and followed her friends through the manor gates happily. As she reached the courtyard Clodagh was greeted by the sight of Ozzie and Merlin standing together with Angela and Dad. Side by side they looked even more alike than Clodagh had realised. She looked in confusion from Dad to Angela and back.

"Well, don't you look amazing," Dad said with a smile.

"Thanks," Clodagh said twirling around. "Hey Ozzie, do you like it?" She rubbed Ozzie's nose and he snuffled at the dress where he thought the pockets should be. "Why do you have him out Dad?" she asked, scratching his neck.

"It was Ma's idea, she found out about the costume and thought you should have at least one picture taken with Ozzie in it," Dad said.

Clodagh wondered how Ma had known about the costume but didn't have time to ask him, as Angela stepped forward holding Merlin.

"And I thought there should be a picture of you with both of these two as well," she said. "Call it a family photo." Clodagh frowned and Angela laughed. "I had a hunch that your Dad confirmed. Clodagh, I'd like you to officially meet Starlight Wizard Warrior, Merlin for short."

"Starlight!" Clodagh gasped. "But, but that's Ozzie's name too! On his passport, he's Starlight Ozwin Legend."

Angela nodded "They're brothers, both out of Starlight Magic and Mythic Soldier Boy. Ozzie is a year older, he's Merlin's big brother. From what I can tell they were at their breeder's together for some time. No wonder Merlin here stuck around the manor." Angela patted Merlin's neck and he snorted at her.

Clodagh smiled broadly and instinctively hugged Merlin, who also nuzzled at her dress. "This is so amazing!" Clodagh said. "I can't believe it!"

"Believe it," Dad said. "We checked the passports. So, shall we take a few photos?"

Clodagh nodded. "But, can we take a group photo too? With everyone?"

Dad smiled. "Of course, we can. Come on you lot, gather around, we'll get the manor in the background."

Clodagh found herself standing between Ozzie and Merlin, with her friends gathered around. Dad pulled out his big camera and started to take a few pictures of them all standing together. It seemed like a dream. It hadn't been so long ago that there had been no horses at the manor, life had been simple and dull. Now, here she was standing next to the most amazing pony, her pony. She looked at her friends gathered in front of the manor and couldn't help but think things were perfect.

"You should take a photo on Ozzie!" Beth said.

"Yeah," Rachel agreed. "That would be so cool!"

Clodagh smiled and led Ozzie over to the mounting block. Climbing up the stone steps she looked down at Ozzie gleaming in the moonlight as she slid onto his back. She turned him around and Dad took a few pictures of her sitting on him.

"Now that's some picture." Clodagh looked up in surprise to see Nick Padget walking across the courtyard towards her. He wore a long green velvet cloak and a brown tunic woven with leaves. On his head sat a twig and leaf crown. There was no doubt in Clodagh's mind that this was his Oberon costume from the theatre.

"Nick, you're, you're Oberon." She smiled.

"Someone had to be!" he smiled, taking her hand. Dad snapped a picture and Ozzie took a test nibble on one of the leaves but quickly realised it wasn't real and let it go, making Nick laugh.

"Ash said someone suggested there should be a Lady Lilly and an Oberon at the party. And here we are." He smiled at Clodagh.

"Me?" she said. Nick smiled and nodded.

"You. You even have the horse," he smiled.

"Wait, you brought the dress. You're the guest in the farm!" Clodagh said.

"Guilty," Nick smiled. "But I'm not the mastermind behind this." He glanced at Ash who smiled broadly and then shrugged.

"That is some planning," Angela said. She smiled. "You ride, don't you?" she asked Ash, and he nodded. "Humm. How about one more picture."

A few minutes later Clodagh found herself sitting on Ozzie stood next to Nick, with Ash sitting on Merlin on the other side of him. Dad took a few more shots and then Clodagh slid down off Ozzie. She led him back to the box next to Dancer and popped him inside with a hug.

"I'd best get Merlin here loaded up," Angela said and everyone gathered around to say goodbye. The little Ozzie look-alike seemed to love all the attention.

"Let's go inside," Sam said as Angela led Merlin away towards the wagon.

"Ok, but maybe we should put Ozzie and Dancer out first, it'll be quieter for them." Clodagh pointed out.

"I'll do it," Dad said. "I've got to nip home and change anyway. You all go on it."

"Thanks Dad," Clodagh smiled.

Ash and Melissa took Clodagh's arms and they turned towards the manor door, following Sam and Beth, with Mike and Alice behind. Nick offered his arm to Rachel and she giggled as she took it and he escorted her inside.

The way down into the cellar had been lit by a series of fake candles hung onto the wall, their light flickering a little, casting shadows on the sandstone. Clodagh stepped down carefully so she didn't trip on the long red skirts of her dress.

Clodagh had been concentrating on getting down the steps so much, it wasn't until they were at the entrance of the cellar that she got her first proper look at it. She gasped. The old trestle tables they had brought down had been hidden under heavy fabric before being loaded with lots of great-looking food. Here there were no labels suggesting the foods were spooky. No, they had gone for a more medieval idea with roast hams, cheeses, bread, and pitches of cider and apple juice. More fake candles had been put in niches and on sconces hung on the wall and there was music playing from the hidden system.

"This is amazing," Nick said with a smile. "Truly, I have been to many a party, but this, well done."

*

An hour later everyone had arrived. Mrs. Fitz had handed over Zeus and Troy and entered to cheers and applause from all the guests. Dad and Ma had both turned up in costume, Dad as a scarecrow and Ma as a mermaid. Sam had been put in charge of the music and had put together a list of fun Halloween-themed songs. Clodagh glanced at him showing Beth how to do the monster mash, she was laughing so hard that some of her lemonade spilled from her cup and Clodagh giggled.

The guests from the manor and B&B mingled together with a few friends who had been invited. She saw Ash standing with Melissa and Nick talking with some of the manor guests. They looked thrilled to be standing with them. Clodagh smiled as Farmer Bob waved at her from across the room and wandered over. He'd dressed up as Hagrid from Harry Potter and Clodagh was impressed with the result, trying not to giggle as he got closer.

"You like it?" he asked, looking at the costume. "Was the wife's idea."

"It's perfect," Clodagh smiled. "You really look like him!"

"Thanks," he said with a proud smile. "Your costume is pretty impressive too, that's a fantastic dress." Clodagh smiled. "Everyone is loving the party; the decorations are amazing."

"Aren't they!" Clodagh said looking around.

"Oh, is that your Ma's roast ham?" he asked spying on the joint on the table. Clodagh nodded with a smile. "Might just get a bit, catch you later." He shuffled off towards the table. Clodagh wondered if she should go and get a plate of food too.

"Hey," Rachel caught her arm. "I saw you eyeing the food, come on." She half dragged Clodagh to the table and grabbed two plates, handing one to her. "Sam said the music is going to be a bit more dance-ey in a bit."

Clodagh took some food and headed off to one side of the room where they had set up a few chairs. She sat next to Rachel and they ate, listening to music and watching the party unfold. Rachel had been right, soon enough the music on Sam's playlist began to change to more upbeat, less Halloween-themed songs and a few people began to dance. Melissa charged over to them with a huge smile on her face, dragging Ash with her. She caught hold of Rachel's hand.

"Come dance," she said, "you too Clodagh!"

"Sorry about this," Ash grinned.

Clodagh and Rachel stood and Melissa dragged them all onto the makeshift dance floor they had set out. Soon enough everyone else seemed to have joined them and they all began to dance together. Nick ended up in the middle and everyone began to laugh as he started doing a few silly dance moves. He caught hold of Clodagh's hands and spun her around making her laugh before Ash caught hold of her and Nick swept up Rachel for his next twirl. Clodagh laughed as she and Ash watched.

The dancing and laughter went on for hours before things started to grow quieter. Sam and Beth were slow dancing along with Mike and Alice. Rachel had almost fallen asleep in the corner of the room by the time Mel had turned up to take her home, she'd hugged everyone before they'd headed off, promising to come over and help clear up in the morning. Mrs. Fitz had already headed to bed leaving Dad to lock the gates when everyone finally left. Melissa and Nick were talking in the corner and eating a few left-over bits on the table that Ma hadn't wrapped up yet.

"Hey," Ash smiled nudging Clodagh.

"Hey." She smiled.

"This was a great party."

Clodagh nodded sleepily. "Yeah, but I think I'm ready to go home now."

"You want me to walk you? I think the others are going to be here a bit longer," he said. "To be honest, I'm pretty wrecked too."

Clodagh smiled and nodded. "I'll let Ma know we're going back; I think she has a few bags of food to take down too if you don't mind helping."

"Sure," Ash said with a grin.

Clodagh gathered the cool bags Ma had packed with leftovers, handing one to Ash and shrugging the other over her shoulder. They said goodnight to everyone left at the party and climbed the stone steps to the main hallway.

Outside in the courtyard, it was decidedly cooler and Clodagh shivered a little. Ash took his cloak off and handed it to her.

"Won't you be cold?"

"Nah, it was way too warm down there for me," he grinned.

They wandered over the courtyard and through the double gates. Without saying a word, they both turned towards the paddock, as if it was the most natural way to go. The paddock was bathed in silver Halloween moonlight. Clodagh pulled open the wicket gate and she and Ash slipped in, closing the little metal gate with a clink behind them.

Ozzie and Dancer were stood together in the top corner, both looked up and Ozzie wandered over to them. He stood next to Clodagh looking out over the paddock as if wondering what she and Ash were looking at. Gently he nudged the bag and she rubbed his cheek.

A low mist clung to the bottom half of the paddock, covering the grass, it was eerily beautiful and Clodagh sighed. A grey cloud passed over the moon, blocking its light for a minute and as it drifted clear Clodagh frowned, the mist almost looked like it had formed the shape of a woman riding on a horse, though the mount's legs were nothing but vapour. She gasped and looked at Ash. He was staring down the paddock too, his eyes wide.

"Did you see..." he trailed off.

Clodagh smiled and scratched at Ozzie's neck. "Yeah, I did." She absently reached out and took hold of Ash's hand, while simultaneously pulling Ozzie just a little closer. They stood staring together as the fog shifted and whatever they had seen drifted away into the woods. Clodagh realised it was midnight, Halloween was ending and it had been the most perfect night. With a smile at Ash, the three headed off down the paddock together. It had been an eventful ending to half term and Clodagh wondered what adventures they'd have before next Halloween. One thing was for sure, with Ozzie around she wasn't afraid to find out.

You did it...

Congratulations! You finished this book.

Loved this book? Consider leaving a review! Book reviews are a valuable way for you to help me share this book about Ozzie and Clodagh with the world. If you enjoyed this book, I would love it if you could leave a review online. Ozzie & Clodagh say a big thank you too!

Enjoy the first book in the new Coral Cove Series at

www.writtenbyelaine.com

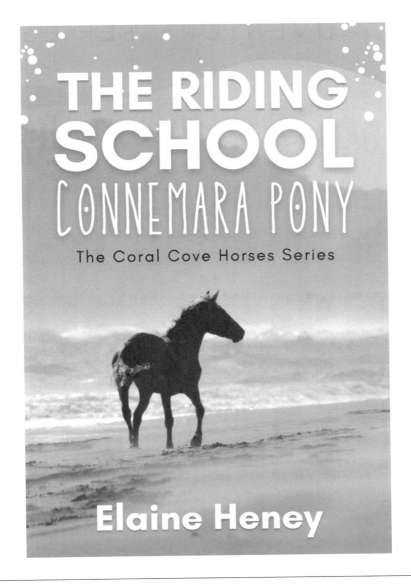

THE
CONNEMARA
ADVENTURE SERIES

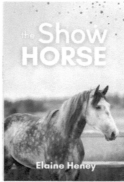

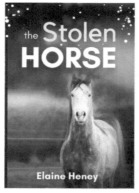

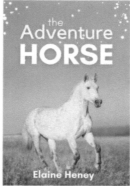

EDUCATIONAL HORSE BOOKS FOR KIDS...

www.writtenbyelaine.com

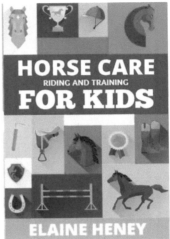

THE CORAL COVE SERIES

www.writtenbyelaine.com

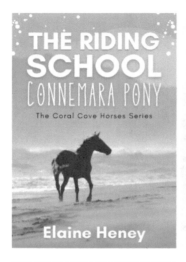

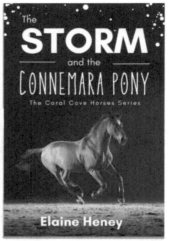

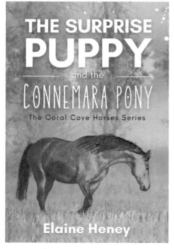

HORSE BOOKS

For teens & adults

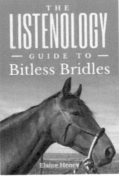

Horse Training Resources

Discover our series of world-renowned online groundwork, riding, training programs and mobile apps. Visit Grey Pony Films & learn more: www.greyponyfilms.com Find all Elaine's books at www.writtenbyelaine.com